**One man has to break the rules...
the other must discover who he truly is.**

Braden Craig is a popular schoolteacher in Gray Vale, and unlike most wolf shifters, he's one of life's peacemakers. When old tensions rise in the newly merged pack, he's quick to douse the flames. But nothing can cool the heat inside him when he locks eyes with the giant blond stranger who has become the target of some less than welcoming packmates' aggression.

Tragedy pushed Marius Voss out of his so-called comfort zone in Stoke Ridge. After being forced to move to Gray Vale with his young son, and still recovering from life-altering injuries, he just wants to keep to himself and figure out his new life. He never expected to find an ally at all, let alone a man like Braden.

When fate plays a hand, and the two men find their lives intertwined, will they find a way to be together?

His Wounded Warrior

Gray Vale Pack

Book Two

Copyright © 2023 Evie Riley

Second Edition

ISBN: 978-1-77357-690-9

Naughty Nights Press LLC

Cover Art By Willsin Rowe

HIS WOUNDED WARRIOR

GRAY VALE PACK

BOOK TWO

EVIE RILEY

CHAPTER ONE

Braden

STANDING BEFORE THE bright and shiny faces of my 2nd Grade students, I savored that bittersweet and beautiful pain that always came at the end of the last day of school.

Even I sometimes found it strange how much at home I felt in the company of kids. Especially for a man with no real chance of ever being a father. I can only put it down to my own family's strong support. The fact they never insisted I take any predetermined path was, in the end, what led me to teaching.

One of the things I loved most about teaching these early grades was that I got to know the kids long before any of them had experienced shifting. There was such a sweetness to them at these ages, and I'd never tire of it. They had some of the senses, of course, since we're all born with them. But they were such perfect little creatures, all singular of mind and being.

With all the eager little faces shining up at me, we performed my own little classroom ritual of gazing at the clock, counting down the last ten seconds until the final bell rang.

HIS WOUNDED WARRIOR

Right on cue, it sounded, and we all cheered. The kids, their parents, me... even Kayleigh, the school principal.

I'd still see these wonderful kids around, of course—in town over the summer break, and around the school in years to come—but there was always that sense of something wonderful coming to an end when school finished for the year.

This had been my best year of teaching, though it wasn't as if I had a huge history to compare with. I was six years into it, but every year still felt as fresh as my first.

Now that Gray Vale had completed the long process of amalgamation with Stoke Ridge, there was an even greater sense of anticipation for the coming school year.

Nothing much had changed, in a day-in, day-out sense, in the two years since the great upheaval. We all just had to remember that Fiona Blair bore the lumpy and cumbersome title of *United Clans Custodian*, rather than the more traditional *Alpha*.

In a couple months' time, though, we'd be welcoming a new intake of people none of us knew. That was such a rarity in wolf clans. Everyone knew everyone, with only rare exceptions. Exceptions like Kayleigh, one of the few humans living in Gray Vale.

I stood by the classroom door, saying goodbye to all the kids in turn, and their parents. Mostly moms, a lot of whom were regulars at my weekly life drawing classes.

Little Tommy Welsh held up his hand for a high five as he passed, and I returned it. His mom, Lillian, touched my arm as she came to a stop in front of me.

She was one of the most persistent flirts I'd ever known, even though she was fully aware of my sexuality.

"Braden, will we see you tomorrow night?"

"Um… sorry?"

"Life drawing? We have to *submit* our final piece, right?"

There was no missing the emphasis she put on the word *submit,* but I glossed over it. Lillian lost her mate not long after Tommy was born. She'd found solace in my art classes, and I was certain she'd blurred the lines I'd always drawn between myself and my students. She'd even gone so far as to offer to pose for me.

In private.

"That's right, Lillian. I look forward to seeing yours."

"Hey, at least buy me a drink first,

handsome." She delivered the come on with just enough smirk and wink to let it exist as nothing more than a joke. But enough sincerity to let me know the offer was well and truly on the table, if I was down for it.

Which I wasn't.

I felt for her, of course. It was a huge part of who I was, after all, to empathize with others. But I'd known since childhood I was gay, even before I knew what being gay meant.

I caught Kayleigh's eye, and made my *come and fucking rescue me* face. To her credit, she hustled right over and stood with me, defusing the flirtations immediately. None of the moms ever risked it when my protector was around.

"Y'know, Braden," she murmured. "All this would stop if you'd mate up."

"Mate up? You're seriously going with *mate up?* Like being alone is a fashion choice?"

"With guys your age, it usually is." She helped me see out the last of the parents, and then closed the door and leaned back against it. It was almost as if she was blocking anybody coming back in.

"So, next year," she said, bugging her big brown eyes and making them stand out against her rich, dark skin. That's how I knew she had bad news. "I have to switch you to kindergarten."

"I was really hoping to stick with 2nd Grade."

"We have at least a half-dozen new kids coming in from the other mob."

"Stoke Ridge was a clan, like ours. Not a mob. Anyway, you're human. You shouldn't have any of the baggage."

Normally, I'd tell a human they didn't have the right, but Kayleigh had earned it. She was as much a part of the old Gray Vale as anybody born here.

She flipped her hand in dismissal. "Anyway. I think it's important to these kids to have a positive male role model in their first year."

"And the fact I'm a *gay* positive male role model?"

"Well, that's more for the parents. They need to get the hang of things in these parts."

"Great. I get to be a token."

She threw her hands onto her broad hips as quickly as a gunfighter. "Is that sass?"

I hung my head to hide my grin. "No, ma'am."

"Sounded like sass. You know there's

only one place I'll let you sass me, Braden Craig."

"Which reminds me, your final piece is due this week."

She put on the most amazing pout. "Aw, teach... can't I have an extension?" She even made her voice into the most annoying teenage whining sound I'd ever heard.

"Sorry, Ms Powell. No can do."

"But teeeach..."

"Do I have to have a word with your parents, young lady?"

She chuckled along with me, then poked me in the chest. "So listen, when the hell are you getting us a *male* model to draw? It's been nothing but T and A. Very beautiful T and A, but a girl got *needs*, y'know?"

"A boy has 'em, too, lemme tell ya. And

if you can find me a guy in the whole of this jambalaya of clans who'll do it, you let me know, huh?"

"You telling me you can't even get one of your exes? I never met anyone before who could stay friends with every single person they got jiggy with."

"My exes? Not a good idea. It sends the wrong message, don't you think?"

She shrugged in defeat. "Shit, it shouldn't be that hard. I never met a shifter could keep his pants on more than ten minutes at a time. This place is junk city." She gave me a hefty hip-check. "Why you think I never left?"

"It's not the nudity that bothers them. It's the standing still."

"Oh, yeah. Not exactly a strong point among your kind. There's always a new sound or scent wafting around."

I hip-checked her back again. "And with all you thirsty females gazing on them, there'd be scents a-plenty, for sure."

"Now why you gotta call me out like that, boy?"

"Because you gave me kindergarten next year." I heard the self-doubt in my own voice, and there was no doubt Kayleigh heard it, too. She never would have lasted among shifters if she didn't have such good instincts.

"B, you're gonna ace it. I've seen you in action."

I still had my doubts. But having the support of my principal helped, at least.

CHAPTER TWO

Marius

THE ESTATE AGENT worked the key into the apartment door and jiggled it.

"It's got a real personality, this one," he said, and though his back was to me, I could hear in his voice the foolish grin he wore. A disturbingly brittle crack sounded, and then he drew open the door and stood aside.

"There we go."

I raised one eyebrow as I glanced inside. My son leaned into my leg and I reached down, ready to put my hand on his shoulder, then held back.

"It smells funny, dad," Noah murmured.

The estate agent—Carl—put on his showiest chuckle. "Oh, it's just the cleaning agents, kiddo. You guys are Ridgies, right?"

"There's no Stoke Ridge anymore," I growled out, not meaning to sound quite so bitter about it.

Carl's canned grin slipped a little, but he recovered quickly enough. "Well, not in name, of course. But we have our own brands we use here in Gray... well, in what we used to call Gray Vale."

That sounded like nothing so much as

complete bullshit to me.

Did this guy really think he could fool a fellow shifter when it came to smells?

"C'mon, let me show you inside."

I just about had to drag Noah with me to get him in. Couldn't blame the kid. I was still a stranger to him. A stranger who happened to be his biological father.

Inside, the place was everything I'd expected. Bland, worn, tattered. But fuck, it was all I could afford. Couldn't serve in the guards anymore, but hadn't served long enough for a decent pension.

At least there were two bedrooms, so Noah could hide his tears from me if he wanted to.

"Why can't we live in mom's house?"

"C'mon, Noah. We've been through that."

Carl coughed, to edge himself back

into the conversation. "Uh, I was told it was just the two of you? If there's a Mrs. Voss...?"

"There's not," I said, more of a snarl than a statement.

"Mom's dead." The antiseptic way Noah said that, every single time, hurt me much more than it would if he showed the slightest sadness. It was like he'd had an emotional bypass.

The apartment went silent for a moment. Carl was so neutral, his façade so false, I couldn't even tell for certain whether he truly was a shifter, or just a human. Especially, when I factored in that cleaning agents crap he tried to spin.

Carl seemed unsure how to proceed at the news of Kellie's death. The look on his face told me he was wondering if I'd killed her. I saw that look all the time. My size, and the way I radiated such clear and obvious *fuck you* vibes, worked well in the guards. Now I couldn't wear the uniform. I was just a huge, messed up guy with some real angry injuries.

"Car accident," I said. "She died in a car accident."

"Oh. And is that where you, um..." He nodded toward my left arm. What there was of it, anyway. I raised it and looked at the short stump below my elbow. I did an exaggerated double take.

"What the hell? It was there a minute ago."

"Um..."

Noah let out a little giggle. It was the only way that I'd ever made the kid laugh, but it was definitely a dad joke. It probably had about two more weeks before he was sick of hearing it. It'd been two months since I got sick of saying it.

I picked up a vibe from Carl that he'd rather be anywhere else, so I held out my good hand, palm up. "We'll take it."

The guy handed over the keys. "Great. And let me know if you ever need a hand with... uh... I mean..." He licked his lips and checked his watch. "If you need any help."

I walked Carl back outside, then brought the bags in one by one. By the time I was done, Noah had claimed his bedroom.

I stood at his door, gazing in on him for a moment. He was small for his age anyway, but in this strange room, in a place we'd never been before, he was hunched over into himself so much it was like he'd shrunk.

"Hey, uh..." I'd been going to call him

son, but that word still caught in my throat. Truth was, I'd planned never to have kids. Last thing I wanted was to dump all my baggage on a child.

But a child happened anyway, and out of fear and uncertainty, I'd let Noah get away from me for years. In the guards, there'd always been another clan to fight, another training session. The fact I'd never been with his mom in any formal way—just physically—hadn't helped me bond with my son.

"Noah? How about we head out and see what's what?"

"'kay."

"I saw something going on in the town square. Big crowd. Maybe we can get to know a few people."

"'kay."

Truthfully, I'd be happy to stay a

stranger to them all. It wouldn't be so different to where I'd been living back in the old Stoke Ridge. Weird that a guy as big as me could be as good as invisible. Then again, I'd done all I could to keep things that way.

But I had to face the truth. Without contacts, I'd be lucky to get any work. And rent wouldn't pay itself.

Noah slid off his bed and came over to me. He took my hand freely enough but there was no real strength or feeling in his grip. I thought about picking him up and putting him on my shoulders, but it felt like too big a move.

Too soon.

Thing is, I loved the kid like crazy. Always had, from the moment he was born. I'd just never known how to show it, let alone how to say it. But when his mom was taken so suddenly, I swore I wouldn't let anybody else write Noah's story, the way mine got written.

The foster system had been tough enough for me, and I'd always been a big motherfucker, even at Noah's age. Of course, that painted a target on my forehead for all the little dogs who wanted to fight the big dog. A kid like Noah would have been chewed up and spat out within a week.

I'd had to fight Kellie's parents for custody, which was a shock to them. They'd never even known of my existence until their daughter's funeral. Apparently she'd told them Noah was from a one night stand and she never actually knew the guy.

Which was a whole lot closer to the truth than I liked to think about. Couldn't blame Kellie for that, either. I was never mean to her, but that didn't mean I was good to her.

Or *for* her.

But in this beautiful little boy, I saw a chance for redemption. Right my own wrongs, and heal the hurts life had already piled on him.

I was probably the least qualified man on earth to raise a kid... but I was his only hope.

CHAPTER THREE

Braden

EVEN THOUGH WE weren't officially a single clan anymore, Gray Vale still existed as a concept. And as a town, we'd decided to keep things running as smoothly as we could.

In this first week of summer break, that always meant it was time for the Country Fair. And for me, that meant setting up my tent and scrawling caricatures of anyone who wanted them.

My skills were far more suited to fine art than cartooning, so my caricatures were only fair to middling. People didn't seem to mind, though. Especially, when all the earnings were being pumped back into the school arts program.

It was the only time I could actually get a male shifter to pose for me, simply because it wasn't serious, and it never took long. It also played into our kind's natural egotistical tendencies. Even when I made fun of a feature, or a personality trait, all that did was let the subject feel more seen. Maybe even understood.

I was halfway through a portrait of Conall Blair, brother of our Alpha-who's-not-an-Alpha, when I caught the scent of trouble. Conall obviously noticed it as well, and he stood immediately. It was clear his guard instincts still ran strongly through his veins.

We glanced across to where the low but urgent voices were coming from. Conall looked ready to shift, but his partner, Zoltan, placed a hand on his shoulder.

"Con, you're a civilian now. Remember?"

"I can't just sit back and let shit go down."

"We have guards for that."

I moved up beside them and tried to work out what was happening. All I could see was a circle of our guys—off duty guards, all of them—and an untamed head of mid-blond hair protruding above all of them. Big guy, obviously, but outnumbered four to one.

I turned to Conall and Zoltan. "I'll get this one, guys."

"Seriously, Braden," Conall growled. "You don't have any guard training."

"I don't have any scars, either."

"So?"

I gave him my calmest, most disarming smile. "So obviously, nobody's ever seen reason to smack the shit out of *me*."

Before he could reply, I strolled over, easing myself through the crowd. It was an ambitious move on my part, sure, but I'd known Conall for years. I'd trust the guy with my life, and choose him to fight on my behalf any time.

The problem was, this was the Country Fair, and fighting was the exact opposite of what we needed. This thing, whatever was happening, was just a little... spot fire.

And Conall Blair was gasoline on legs.

As I reached the small mob, I realized the guy in the center was a stranger.

But holy hell, what a man.

A little older than me, taller even than Conall, and broader in the shoulders. There was no missing the trauma on his left arm, since the lower half was, itself, missing. His square, rugged face bore scars of battle, but his aura was even more scuffed up and broken.

"Come on, then," he growled, looking from one man to the next. I found it impossible to look away from him. It was more than just how goddamn sexy the guy was. He radiated all the isolation and brittle aggression of a stray dog.

And I'd always had a thing for strays.

"Fuckin' Ridgie," one of our guys said, and spat on the grass. "Yeah, I recognize you. There can't possibly be two fuckers as big and ugly as you. Only last time, you were better... *armed.*"

The speaker took a step forward, and the big guy's entire bearing changed. The Gray Vale guys were too invested in hating him to see clearly, but from my place as an observer, it was plain as day.

If this thing played out, then I had no doubt there'd be only one man standing by the end of it. This damaged but determined giant.

The other off-duty guards moved in as well, and the stranger glanced down toward the ground. Only then did I see the kid with his eyes wide with fear, clinging to the man's tree trunk leg.

That was all I needed to get stung into motion.

"Fellas," I said, grabbing a couple of

our guys on their shoulders as I glided between them. "What seems to be the trouble here?"

"Fuck off, Braden. This isn't your concern."

"Oh, come on. Just think about what you're saying. And the young, impressionable ears you're saying it in front of. Yeah?"

"They've heard worse."

"But you know better." I put myself between the guardsmen and their quarry, facing our guys. Which of course, meant turning my back to the most dangerous man in the situation. "Seriously, guys. This is all kinds of messed up."

"What do you care? This asshole—" He jabbed his finger at the guy behind me. "Fought against us for years."

"Us?"

"Gray Vale."

"Then it's a good thing we're all one big happy family now, isn't it?"

"What would you even fucking know about it, Braidy-Cat? You ever done anything real with your life?"

"Everything I do is real, Simon."

"What, drawing your stupid cartoons? Playing dress-ups with children?"

I knew he was just trying to get under my skin. Thing was, I was beyond used to it. I'd taught *their* kids, for fuck's sake.

"Your boy Billy loved dress-ups. Always wanted to play at being a Gray Vale guard. *I'm gonna be just like my daddy,* he'd say." I leaned a little closer. "You think he'd be saying that right now?"

Simon visibly relaxed at the mention of his kid. I guess that counted as my biggest talent. Defusing bombs.

As a last shot across the bows, he pointed at the big beast of a man behind me. "You just keep out of my way, you hear?"

"Wasn't in your way to begin with, sunshine."

God, even the guy's voice was sex on legs. Deep and sonorous, with more than a hint of sharpness in there. The sound of it so close behind me took my mind to all kinds of places. Places I really shouldn't be going in public, even when it was only inside my head.

The guardsmen dispersed and all ambled away, making sure to stare menacingly back at the big man. I let myself relax a little, right up until the guy spoke again.

"Didn't need your help, y'know."

I turned to face him, and bit down on

my tongue. I mean, *damn*. Every single part of him sang to me, in ways that really never happened. In my experience, anyway. His scent filled my nose like his profile filled my eyes, like he would no doubt fill me in every other way.

Except, there was also no doubt that kid was his, and that, of course, meant the big, beautiful guy wasn't even playing for my team.

I let my mouth venture into a tiny grin. "You did, y'know? Need my help. Not in the way you meant it, but you sure did."

He stood a little straighter, his whole aura galvanizing. "What? You think I couldn't have taken those old guys down? There were only four of them."

Still with my peacemaking smile, I shook my head. "That's not what I meant. I'm talking about first impressions here.

Just 'cause we're all shifters doesn't mean we have to be animals about it."

"You sure about that? Comes with the territory."

I shrugged off his comment. "For some, maybe. Those who are all about the strength and not the senses. They hide the tongue behind the teeth."

We stood in silence for a few seconds while he put in some work on deciding whether I was any kind of threat to him. Or just some hippy-dippy nobody.

"Well," I said, and held out my hand to him. "Since we're currently human, I should observe the customs. My name's Braden Craig."

He raised his eyebrows just the tiniest amount. To the eye alone, it probably looked like surprise. With the added depth of shifter senses, I could see it was more confusion than anything. I was more used to that reaction than I cared to admit.

He finally reached out and took my hand. "Marius Voss. And this is my son, Noah."

I dropped to one knee and held my hand out to the kid. "How are you, Noah?"

The kid flashed a smile at me, made brighter by being so brief. He took my hand and I feigned agony.

"Hey, hey, don't squeeze so tight, man."

That drew a proper chuckle from the kid, and his whole face came to life.

Of more interest to me was his father's reaction. Marius drew his head back ever so slightly. It was almost certainly nothing more than surprise, but the motion had all the appearance and feel of a flinch.

I stood again, and reached out slowly toward Noah. Giving him, and his sex-on-legs father, all the chances in the world to stop me. When neither of them did, I ruffled his blond mop, eliciting another small laugh.

"So," I began. "You're from the *enemy*, huh?" I made sure to say it with a smile.

To my relief, Marius smiled back. A genuine, though tiny, grin. And fuck me if the man didn't just light up, in exactly the same way as his kid had.

This was not good.

He was far from the first straight man I'd fallen instantly in lust with, but all the others had at least been single and childless.

"Yeah," he said, his voice deep and soft. "Stoke Ridge, born and bred. As far as I'm aware."

Noah jiggled around from foot to foot. "Dad, I'm bored."

"Hey, young man," I said. "How'd you like me to draw a caricature of you?"

He stared at me like I'd spoken a whole other language, so I bent to his level again. "It's sort of like a cartoon. You like cartoons?"

Noah looked up to his father for reassurance. I did the same, looking for permission. Marius lightly patted the kid's shoulder and nodded at me.

"Y–yes," Noah said, barely more than a whisper.

"Come on over, then."

CHAPTER FOUR

Marius

I'D BEEN READY to take on all four of those assholes. Being outnumbered was par for the course in my life. From the moment way, way back when my father was killed, it'd been me against the world.

Moving here to Gray Vale, where we'd so long been the enemy, I'd expected to be the odd one out. And for as long as it took.

What I hadn't expected was to find an ally. And not a brother-in-arms, like I'd have expected, but a damn peacemaker. I got the feeling this Braden guy could be a whole lot more.

Maybe even a friend.

My first impression was that he had a broad smile that was always right there below the surface. It was as if his mouth could shapeshift, too. He could draw that smile out as quick as an old-time gunfighter with his pistol. Only in his case, it seemed to disarm everyone around him.

Including me.

As soon as Braden stepped into the mix, he cooled the entire situation. That was a kind of talent I couldn't remember ever seeing before.

HIS WOUNDED WARRIOR

He led us over to his stall. It was little more than a tent with the sides rolled up. A picnic blanket on the grass below it, an easel at one corner, and a stool at the opposite.

"Why don't you sit there, Noah?" he said.

My son looked at me again, and all that did was remind me how little I knew the kid. We'd been in forced proximity now for a few weeks. Intense, inescapable togetherness, which still hadn't managed to break down any barriers.

"Go, son. It's fine."

Noah got onto the stool, and it was just like it had been in the apartment, when he sat on his new bed. With his back bent and his head bowed, it was as if he was trying to take up the absolute minimum of space.

It showed up most when he was in a position like this. Out in the open, the focus of attention. Even when that attention was only from me, and this Braden guy.

"Sit up straight, son," I said, trying to keep my voice neutral.

Noah jolted upright so quickly he almost fell back off the stool. I hated the way that looked. The way I imagined it would look to Braden. Like the kid was scared shitless by his own father.

Fuck, that probably wasn't too far from the truth, if I was honest. But when it was out on display like that, for anyone to see, it cut me deep. Because no matter the truth, it would be easy for people to think the worst of me. That I spoke with my hands.

Well, *hand.*

HIS WOUNDED WARRIOR

Finding the right balance was the hardest part of parenting for me. All my examples were at the extreme ends. A father killed in the line of duty, a mother who lost her shit and abandoned me, and foster parents who either ignored me or smothered me—in one case, literally.

All I really had was my training in the guards, and the only thing that had going for it was consistency. It served its purpose, and helped mold me, but it was also what led to me being the physical and mental wreck I now was. No way I could use that shit for raising my son.

If Braden thought anything negative, he kept it well hidden. Standing at his easel, he flashed that incredible smile again, and it had the exact same effect on Noah that it had on those assholes before. My son's posture, his whole bearing, relaxed.

"So, Noah," Braden said. "What do you like doing?"

"Um..." My son looked at me again, as if I had an answer. I wished I did, and I knew I should, but recreation just hadn't been a feature in our lives, yet. Too busy just trying to keep ourselves one step ahead of chaos.

Again, Braden didn't seem flustered. The guy clearly had some skills with kids, and I couldn't help envying him. But at the same time I was more than grateful. He put out an aura that my wolf responded to in ways that... well, frankly, ways that confused me. Like he could become even more than just a friend.

A confidante.

A brother.

Braden rubbed his chin as he made a

big show of studying my son. "So, too many things you like doing, and you can't nail it down. I see that a lot. You like riding bikes?"

Noah lowered his head again. I'd never been there so far to teach the kid how to ride. I doubted his mother ever did, either.

Kellie had never been into the outdoors. In some bizarre way, I think that's what drew me to her in the first place. She was the opposite of what most shifters were like. And suddenly, I realized that Braden had some of that same energy about him. He gave off a real vibe of being an indoorsman all the way. Which was another factor that made me wonder why I felt an instant kinship with him.

"Well, maybe I can draw you on a bike anyway. Whaddya say, kiddo?"

Noah raised his head again, his face all lit up with excitement, like I'd never seen it before. "Yes, please."

"Awesome." Braden disappeared behind his huge sketchbook, popping out every few seconds to take another look at Noah. The scratching of his pencil against the paper seemed like the only sound, despite the bustling fair going on around us.

"And what about music, Noah? You like music?"

My son nodded unconvincingly, reminding me of the bare bones nature of our shared life. Music was yet another pleasure that had escaped us as we scrabbled desperately just to find a foothold.

Right here and now, though, there was a great sense of belonging. I wondered if we might have found our forever home. Not that shitty apartment, of course, but the town of Gray Vale.

Braden continued to toss easy and lighthearted questions at my son, and I made sure not to get in the way of it. Noah opened up to this man in ways I could barely believe. I was learning almost as much about the kid as Braden was.

It only took a few more minutes, and then Braden pulled the page off his sketchbook and turned it around to face us.

"Damn," I said, keeping my voice soft. "That's good, man."

"I might not be much of a fighter, but I *see* people. Y'know?" He put his hand on Noah's shoulder. "This young fella likes to hide himself, but I have ways of uncovering a man's true nature."

I looked over the picture again. As promised, he drew Noah on a bike. He captured my son's furtive smile perfectly.

Braden rolled up the picture and handed it to me. I took it, and tucked it under my arm so I could reach out and shake the guy's hand.

"Thanks, Braden. It's been... tough to find my way in over here." I released the handshake and rested my hand on Noah's head. "Until today."

He flashed that megawatt smile of his again. "Don't think you're getting out of it that easy, big guy."

"What are you talking about?"

He pulled the pencil back out from behind his ear and used it to point to the stool. "Your turn, sunshine." He even used the name I called that guard.

I could feel the look on my face. It was

my classic *you gotta be fucking kidding me* expression. To his credit, Braden didn't give an inch. He just took his place at the easel.

"Dad?" Noah said, looking up at me. "I did it. You can do it."

"See?" Braden said with a victory smile. "Noah, you are wise beyond your years, young man."

Between the two of them, they'd sucker punched me. No way I could refuse now. It'd seem rude to the only guy who'd been on my side. And it would be a fresh new way to disappoint my son.

So, I took my place on the stool, feeling more conspicuous than I did when I stood. That, despite being a good three inches taller than almost everyone around me, was all the time.

"Just get comfortable, big guy," Braden

said, once again disarming me with that brilliant smile.

I couldn't even get it straight in my head what *comfortable* would be. I tried leaning forward, then sitting back. I went to cross my arms, momentarily forgetting I was missing half of one of them.

"Hey, Marius?"

"Huh?"

He held up his pencil. "It isn't really mightier than the sword, you know."

It was a pretty lame joke, but as with everything else he'd done so far, it worked.

And for the first time in a long time, I not only felt relaxed... I felt at peace.

CHAPTER FIVE

Braden

FOR A HUGE and sexy guy, Marius looked adorably uncomfortable as he tried to strike a pose. I had no doubt he could wrestle alligators and lift rolled-over cars. It was sitting still and being looked at that made the guy nervous.

"Seriously, man," I said. "Just relax. Nobody's looking. It's just Noah and me here with you."

He frowned as he clenched and opened his fist. "I'm just... I'm used to being invisible."

"Dude, you could be seen from space."

He let out a quiet, humorless chuckle and raised his damaged arm. "This, though. This makes people look away. Or stare right through me."

I let a breath pass before I asked my next question. "So, you want me to draw it back in? Or go more true to life?"

"You're the artist."

That was too vague for me to decide yet, so I started with his face.

His rugged, beautiful face.

As I sketched his strong features, I tried to engage him in conversation. "So, what about you, Marius?" he asked. "What do you like?"

"Huh?"

"Are you a football fan? You like needlepoint? Rollerblading?" I just hoped he understood I was teasing.

He looked completely blank for a moment. "Y'know, I don't think I have a *thing*. Been so wrapped up in adjusting to all the changes in my life."

"You must have had something before all that." Even with shifter senses, I couldn't quite get a read on him. He presented straight as fuck, but there were all kinds of doubts running through him as well. I couldn't be sure none of them were sexual.

"Nothing that matters anymore."

The dull tone of his voice had me feeling the topic was closed for discussion, so I changed tack. Even though I could tell it was a sensitive area,

I hoped he'd open up about his injury.

"So, your arm," I said. Yeah, okay... subtlety wasn't my strong point.

Marius raised one eyebrow, but otherwise remained still.

"You miss it?"

He lifted the damaged limb and looked the scarred stump over. It almost looked like he was seeing it for the first time. "I, uh... well, I've learned how to get along without it, but I wish I'd never lost it. I guess that might count as missing it."

I kept drawing as I absorbed his words, rolling them around in my head to see if I could pick up any of the unspoken ones. Marius seemed used to presenting himself as a vault. Impregnable and unreadable. Like his heart and soul were both more scarred than his arm.

So, again, I tried a disarming side step

in the conversation. "What are your plans, now you've upgraded to Gray Vale?" I made sure to let him see me smiling. What good was a generations-long rivalry if you couldn't poke fun at people about it?

"No plans, yet," he murmured, low enough that humans wouldn't have heard him. "Looking for work, and... well, I guess I should try and get a few, uh..."

I waited for the last word, but it never came. "Friends?"

"Mm. Those." He let out a long, low sigh that took on a little gravel as it rolled along.

I had to clamp my mouth closed to stop myself asking about people who'd be more than friends.

Or friends with benefits.

There was no chance of a future with

Marius, despite how hard I already crushed on him.

He took another breath, and then opened up a little more. "Truth is, this is the most conversation I've had with an adult in... probably, six months."

"Well, I'm honored. And..." I signed my name at the bottom of the caricature. "I'm done."

Noah scurried around to get a look at my work. Marius was a whole lot more circumspect, but when he stood, there was no doubt he'd relaxed a little more. He moved with a cautious grace now, which seemed at odds with his height and bulk.

"Look, dad," Noah said, pointing at the drawing. "It's you."

I stepped back and let Marius see it properly. His expression stayed stony as he looked it over. I was more interested in watching him than studying my work.

One thing I'd picked up as soon as I saw him was that Marius might as well be covered in spikes. He was clearly so hard to get close to. I didn't know his past yet, but I was fully invested in finding it out.

Only thing I felt certain of was that he hadn't let anybody see him—*really* see him—in many years. And it was probably because of however people saw him before that.

Right back into childhood.

So with my caricature, I'd accentuated his size, of course, and the strength of his handsome features.

He raised an eyebrow and looked at me. "What's going on here?" He poked at the illustration, where I had his damaged arm lifted.

"Oh, that," I said, flashing him a tiny smile. "That's just you flipping us all the bird."

"You didn't draw the arm in."

"Didn't think I needed to."

His heavy brows drew together in a deep frown. I suddenly feared for my safety, wondering if I'd misread him. My wolf raised his hackles deep inside, but with a man as fearsome as Marius, I was definitely preparing for flight, and not fight.

He surprised me by simply grunting, and then kneeling beside his son. "What do you think, Noah?"

"It's really good. You look silly but still scary."

I caught the look of pain on the big man's face, though it only lasted a fraction of a second. Marius nodded, then stood again, turning toward me.

"How much do I owe you?"

I waved him away. "No charge." I'd cover it from my own pocket. Strange as it might be to anyone else, I actually felt that I got more out of this whole thing than he did.

"You work for free? Your wife must be very understanding."

That one little sentence gave me a clearer picture of the guy. And especially his experiences with women.

"No wife." I had the choice to leave it at that. Of course, I didn't. "Never was, and never will be."

The fold between his brows deepened. "You don't strike me as a loner, Braden. I see how you are with, uh... y'know."

"People?"

"Mm."

"Well, I'm not. A loner, that is. I'm very popular, even with the ladies. But, uh... the ladies aren't popular with me, if you catch my drift."

He raised both brows instantly as he processed what I'd just told him.

"Huh. Well. Uh..." His whole body language changed instantly. He reverted to that uneasy confusion he'd had when he first sat to pose. As if my confession somehow exposed him.

I couldn't help but take the tiniest bit of hope from that. Maybe there was a chance, however slim, that he'd be open to trying something new.

"But either way," I said, trying to change the subject to stop him thinking too hard, or in the wrong direction. "The drawing is yours."

For a few seconds, he looked

determined to argue. The guy clearly wasn't used to any kind of charity. Maybe he thought it looked weak. Eventually, he nodded his thanks, rolled up the picture and handed it to Noah.

He reached out and I shook his hand, and then he turned to leave. My wolf whined deep inside me, like he hadn't in many a moon. It was more of a warning to my human side than anything else.

"Listen," I started, and Marius turned back. "If you need, uh... y'know, anything? I'm pretty well connected."

Ugh.

That sounded like the lamest pickup line that had ever been tossed out there. And to no avail, of course. After all, widowers did tend to be dudes of the old hetero persuasion. While he didn't run screaming or threaten violence, it was clear my coming out to him also hadn't landed the way I'd dreamed it might.

Marius kinked his head to the side, growled out a quick thanks, and then left.

Without my number, my address, my details, or any way to contact me.

Message received.

CHAPTER SIX

Marius

IT WAS HARD as hell to make sense of this place. When Stoke Ridge was a separate entity, we'd all been taught to sneer at Gray Vale. And one of the chief reasons was their open and accepting culture. Especially when it came to gay folk.

I'd taken that school of thought on

easy enough in the guards. Fuck, it was practically mandatory to hate on anyone who wasn't part of Stoke Ridge. Doubly so for what our rulers determined to be *perverts and sinners.*

Now that I was actually living in Gray Vale, the truth was much simpler. People are people, whoever, wherever, and whatever the fuck they are.

On the other hand, unlike back up on the ridge, at least down here there was *one* person in my corner. I couldn't work out Braden's deal, but my wolf didn't give me any danger signals.

I felt like the world's rudest prick when I left. All the guy did was to offer help, and listen to me. Fuck, he just about yanked some little home truths out of me, without me quite understanding how.

Like a magic show.

He had me concentrating on one thing and suckered me into opening up.

Noah dragged behind me, and I took hold of his hand to keep him with me. I realized I'd been striding at my own speed. Still thinking about Braden. Wishing I'd been brave enough to ask his number, wondering if I should go back and get it. Tail between my legs and whining.

Was I seriously that fucking desperate?

I'd take the first bone anyone tossed me and call it a friendship?

The guy radiated charm, in a way I'd never seen in anybody before. He'd be friends with every fucker in town. Last thing he needs is for the new guy—the big, wounded oaf—to crowd him.

"Dad, you're hurting me."

I glanced down to where Noah's tiny fist disappeared inside mine, and let go like I'd been burned.

Fuck.

That was exactly how I did everything.

Over the top, or not at all.

"Sorry, son."

He looked close to tears, and I held my breath as I tried to figure out what to do.

What had Braden done?

Whatever it was, Noah relaxed around him.

I dropped to one knee, like Braden had. And I reached out for my son, moving my hand slowly. His big eyes bugged in confusion, but he relaxed when I stroked my fingers back through his hair.

"I mean it, Noah. I'm sorry. I got distracted."

"It's okay, dad."

No, son.

It isn't.

I'm your world, and I'm just not big enough or strong enough for the role.

Thank fuck I managed not to spill my thoughts out all over the kid.

"Come up here," I said instead, picking the boy up and sitting him over the back of my neck. "Let's go home."

"To our old house?"

I winced in reaction. Poor kid didn't seem to get how permanent this situation was. "To the new place, son."

"Okay. I like your new friend."

"Who, Braden?"

"Uh-huh."

I gave a brief nod and kept walking. "Yeah. Me, too."

Was *like* a strong enough word,

though?

The guy made me feel stuff. Stuff I didn't feel. Ever. Not with any of the guards, not with any of my foster parents.

In only a matter of minutes, Braden had my head whirling with the kind of thoughts that would get a man whipped back in the old Stoke Ridge. Because whatever it was that Braden awoke inside me, it was closest to how I'd felt right at the start with Kellie.

Except much stronger.

And honestly, that scared the shit out of me. I knew Gray Vale folks had been cool with that kind of thing for generations, now, but I still had my baggage.

***

It was probably for the best that I didn't

get anything more than Braden's name. No address or number, no idea where he worked.

Okay, yeah, so I'd barely stopped thinking about him in the weeks since we met. And sure, I could ask around and find out more about him. Track him down and just see where things might go.

But the fact was, things might go way beyond anything I was prepared for. I'd never been a fearful man. Even against the bear shifter who took my arm, I never backed down.

So why did this one guy have me all torn up inside?

Why couldn't I shake him?

Why the hell hadn't I even entertained the idea of being with any of the women around here?

More than a few had thrown

themselves right into my path, after all.

I kept telling myself my continued celibacy was for Noah's sake. I didn't want to bring any more instability into his life. But the truth was much simpler than that.

Lack of interest.

In the women, in a relationship, in the chaos that always, *always* came with sex. Even casual sex had loud echoes in a place where everyone knew everyone. And Noah was living proof that the most casual encounters still had lifelong consequences.

So I kept rolling through life, putting one foot in front of the other. Making sure Noah at least had all he needed, even if I couldn't give him much of what he wanted. I knew the kid was hurting for some friends but I just didn't have the contacts yet.

But it was finally his first day of school, and surely that would make things better. At least, it'd give me a chance to really look for some work. Something casual to start with, so I could work around Noah's school day.

Our apartment was close enough to the school that we could walk it. When my son's nerves got the better of him, I suppressed my ingrained instinct to bark at him. Tell him to man up, or some equally awful shit. The kind of so-called parenting I'd always had.

Instead, I picked him up, and carried him. Said nothing, just held him close. He snuggled against my neck in a way I couldn't remember him doing before, and it felt as if my heart suddenly woke up.

At the entrance to the school, I put

him back down and walked him in. We followed the crowd through to the hall.

The teaching staff were all lined up on the stage, and all the kids and parents had arranged seating. I stayed up near the back out of habit. Just to stop anyone behind complaining they couldn't see past me.

Once I took my seat, Noah clambered up into my lap. Again, my first instinct was to push him off, onto his own seat. Didn't want people to think he was a mama's boy, or anything.

I managed to push that feeling down. Something I'd grown better and better at in the last few weeks. And all because of Braden, and his natural way of just letting people be their best fucking version of themselves.

Nobody had ever influenced me so

much, in so little time. It dawned on me then that I was an idiot for not looking him up. Trying to connect with him. Maybe now that I'd have more time on my hands, I could try to make a genuine friendship with the guy.

Noah wriggled on my lap and leaned against my chest. The kid was getting closer to me every day, and I had to be honest... I fucking loved it. Even though I was constantly shitting myself that I'd screw him up through inexperience or simply by being myself.

Then my son made a little *ooh* sound, and I glanced down at him in case he was in pain.

"What is it, son?"

"Look. Braden."

"Huh?" I looked around the parents but couldn't see the guy. "Noah, come on.

You gotta stop doing this."

Since that day when we met Braden, Noah had kept insisting he saw the guy everywhere. And he'd never been right. Not once. I thought it must have been wishful thinking, since the two of them hit it off so well.

"I saw him, dad."

I took a breath rather than shoot him down. Another little thing I'd been trying which seemed to work. "Okay, son. I can't see him, though."

Any further discussion was knocked aside by the principal standing up and beginning her welcome speech. We sat through it all, and I paid as much attention as I could.

Honestly, since Noah said the guy's name, all I could think of was Braden.

What the hell was going on with me?

I never got like this over anybody before. Hell, even my wolf was pacing around inside me, licking his lips and whining.

Over a *guy*.

What gives?

Then the school principal cut through my confused inner monologue, by saying the very name I couldn't shift from my head.

"And teaching kindergarten this year, Mister Braden Craig."

Ah, fuck.

He not only worked at my kid's new school, but he was Noah's classroom teacher?

That felt like it really threw a spanner in the works. Sure, we could still be friendly, but somehow that made it seem like we couldn't be *friends*.

Or… anything.

I turned my attention back to the stage and held my breath as the man himself stepped up to the lectern. He was dressed a little more formally than when I saw him at the Country Fair, but he still had that same aura of calm certainty.

Which was the complete opposite of everything that was whirling around inside my mind and my body. A sensation something like a fucking maelstrom of confusion, with a light dusting of—weirdly—happiness.

CHAPTER SEVEN

Braden

I ALMOST HOSED up my welcome speech, and for one reason only.

Marius.

Even when he was seated, and even way up the back, the guy stood out like a hard-on in church.

Or in my case, a hard-on at the lectern. Because just catching a glimpse of him had my cock tingling as it filled and stiffened. I was a damn lost cause.

Why did I so often fall for straight guys?

I seriously thought I had a better brain than that. I probably did, actually. It was just that I was thinking with a whole other part of my anatomy, yet again.

At least I did manage to get through the welcome, and back to my seat, and I didn't think anybody noticed the boner I was sporting.

Of course, I'd known that Noah would be in my class this year. I got the list from Kayleigh a couple weeks back. So, I shouldn't have been surprised to see Marius. He'd be one of "my" parents all year, and we'd no doubt have some time to chat.

Unfortunately, that would be all we

could do.

There weren't exactly rules about this stuff, but there was at least a strong expectation. And that was that we keep our hands off our students' parents.

Even the big, rough diamonds of pure sexiness.

Dammit.

If Noah was in someone else's class, then I could be more friendly with Marius. But the way things were, it was too easy to cross lines that couldn't then be uncrossed. I'd rather look forward to a lifelong friendship with him, starting next year, than to never see him.

Stupid me, I still held out hope that he'd be open to a little one-on-one time with me, sometime down the track. If I had to wait a year, until Noah was in another teacher's class, I could do it. It'd be hard as hell—and so would I—but I'd manage.

Finally, the welcome session was over, and we made our way to our classrooms. I welcomed all the kids into my room, one by one. I noticed that Marius hovered right at the back of the line, and Noah was clutching at his father's muscular leg like he had back at the Country Fair.

It sure seemed I'd have some work to do with that sweet kid. I'd only met him for a short time, but my impression was that he was smart, polite and kind, but that there were some real trust and self-esteem issues whirling around inside him as well.

The pair of them reached the doorway last of all, and though I didn't want to single Noah out for special treatment, I kinda couldn't help myself. For him, I dropped to one knee again and held out my fist.

"Noah. Good to see you again, my man."

The kid looked at my bunched up hand in confusion, then up at his father. Marius made his own fist and pumped it gently forward, and Noah's understanding showed on his sweet face.

He followed his father's example and moved his little hand forward, his fingers barely even curled back. The feather-light touch when his knuckles met mine only seemed to confirm what I'd thought.

Now I really couldn't help myself. I was here for it, whatever *it* was. I wanted to know the back story for what made this adorable kid disappear into himself like he had. The dynamic between son and father wasn't smooth, but there were no warning signs at all.

This man clearly loved his son, but it was kind of like how I love the French language. It takes my breath away with how beautiful it is, and yet I barely understand a word of it.

That was how it looked with Marius. I could see it on his worn but handsome face how much he adored his little man. But it was as if he was constantly searching for the subtitles so he could work out what was going on with the kid.

"Come on in, my man," I said to Noah, and held out my hand to shake with Marius. "Good to see you again, too."

He shook back readily enough.

"Braden. I should have guessed you'd be a teacher."

His voice was just as I remembered it. Volume and pitch low, like he was doing everything possible to be invisible. I swore there were harmonics there that only my wolf could hear. And damn if it didn't just confuse the hell out of both sides of me.

Marius seemed a little easier to get a handle on than his son was. There was a reclusive nature about the man that I was certain had nearly everything to do with his size. After all, that day I'd met him, he'd been the center of attention mostly because he stood out so much.

He must get that kind of shit all the time. Factor in his crunched up arm and it was no wonder he wanted to move through life in the shadows.

Well... not on my watch. Just because I couldn't be with him didn't mean I couldn't hang around him. Force him into some quiet socializing. Not big groups or loud events. Hell, if I had my way they'd be just the two of us.

Sittin' in a tree.

Whether he knew it or not, Marius needed me. Maybe as much as his son did, but in a different way.

***

I knew Noah would need some help easing his way into school life. Not only was it his first year, but he was the only kid in the class who wasn't born and raised in Gray Vale.

To begin with, I cherry-picked a few of the kids whose parents I knew well, and gave Noah some time paired up with them. The kids who were naturally quiet but strong, and whose families had strong bonds.

Within a few days, the gentle and involved attention of the kids—and me—

had Noah coming at least partway out of his shell. It helped that he'd not only shown a great interest in art... he also had some ability. That gave me something to work with outside of regular school stuff.

Over the past couple of weeks, he'd been staying back after school, waiting for his dad to pick him up. Marius always arrived later than most. I never minded since it meant I could get a little time to actually talk to that big, sexy man without interruption. Plus I knew it was one of his coping mechanisms.

There was so much less chance of him having to talk to strangers—the other parents—if he got here after they'd all left. Especially, all those desperately thirsty single moms. Even the married ones were too handsy for my liking. And damn if I hadn't had to run interference on Kayleigh more than once.

Not that I could blame them.

Marius really was something else.

And as much of a thrill as it was to watch Noah begin to blossom, it hit me even harder to see his father opening up to me. Of course, I wasn't naïve enough to think things would ever go beyond friendship. Straight guys are pretty hard to score with, after all.

By the end of the second week, Noah had almost become a brand new boy. He'd settled in beautifully and had a couple of kids he clearly thought of as friends.

He seemed to really appreciate the extra time I took with him, too. As we waited for Marius to arrive, I looked over Noah's latest artwork.

"I love what you're doing here, my

man," I said, and the boy practically wriggled in reaction. Praise still worked magic on him.

"Thank you, Mister Craig."

As usual, he'd drawn a house. A standalone house with a wide pathway. Perhaps a symbol of welcoming, although he rarely actually drew any people in or around the houses. The only times he did, the figures were clearly his father and himself. Nobody else.

The kid still radiated a sense of loss, and a feeling of solitude. I could pick those up almost as well in my human senses as my wolf. Despite how he was becoming more gregarious, he still awoke in me a desire to protect. I lost myself in the moment, and before I thought about it, I rested my hand on Noah's shoulder.

I gave him the lightest little squeeze of

solidarity before taking my hand away. I had to really watch myself there, of course. I'd grown fond of the boy beyond the level a teacher should, and there was no doubt it was in part because of how I felt about his father.

"Are you ready for tonight, Noah?" He'd been invited for a sleepover, and he clearly was beyond keen to go. Still, he shrugged as if it was nothing.

"I have to ask my dad."

I had great hope that Marius would okay the deal. Surely, he could do with a night off as well. I'd learned enough to know that active and involved fatherhood was still relatively new to him.

At that moment, I spotted the man walking in to my classroom to pick up his son. Prowling toward us, moving with natural stealth, radiating peril, and as always, I simply couldn't look away from him.

Once again, I had to push my wolf down. The hunger my inner beast had for this tall, rough man was beyond anything I'd ever known. And it got sharper whenever Marius smiled at me. Like he was doing right at that moment.

"Braden," he said, more of a growl than a word. Then he turned to his son. "Ready to go, Noah?"

"Noah has something he needs to ask you," I blurted, desperate to keep Marius near me for a little longer.

Marius glided down to a crouch to bring himself eye to eye with Noah. "What's up, son?"

The boy didn't look away from his drawing as he spoke. "There's a sleepover tonight. I got invited."

Marius frowned, and looked up at me. "Sleepover. Already?"

"Noah's really getting popular." Marius still looked a little confused, so I pushed a little harder. "I do think it'd be good for him to go."

That seemed to be all Marius needed to make his decision. "Then let's get you home and packed," he said, sounding more playful than I could ever recall.

Noah packed up his drawing and picked up his bag while I gave Marius the details for the sleepover. The big man shook my hand and I soaked up the feel of his skin, his heat, for a moment.

Just as they were about to leave the classroom, he turned back. "Listen, Braden…"

My wolf leapt up inside me, ears pricked, tail poised. On the surface I tried to remain calm. "Yes?"

"I wanted to thank you for... helping us both."

"That's no problem. It's what I do."

He nodded and scratched his jaw. "Yeah, but... it's not something anyone's done for me, before. I was thinking..."

"Hmm?"

"This might be breaking some kind of rule, I guess. But since Noah's gonna be out, maybe you'd like to get together?"

Oh man.

There was nothing I wanted more.

"It's not against any rules," I said, though I wasn't completely sure I was right about that. "But like... beers at the tavern kind of thing?"

He screwed his face up at that idea. "I was more thinking of dinner. I have a couple steaks thawed, and maybe we can... y'know. Talk about Noah's progress."

That wasn't quite what I wanted, but fuck it.

I'd take it.

"I'd love to."

CHAPTER EIGHT

Marius

I KNEW WHEN I invited Braden in that I was overstepping. Moving outside my comfort zone. But he'd been so good with Noah, helping my son adjust to the new town, to the daunting experience of starting school.

The guy had been pretty much the perfect blend of teacher, father, and even mother to my son. I still didn't really get how socialization worked, but when it came to Braden, I wanted to make a real effort. Even if all I could do to start with was mimic what I saw others doing.

That was why I'd extended the invitation. That was why he was sitting here at the dining table, across from me, savoring the basic-ass dinner I made for him.

Or so I told myself.

"This is really good, Marius."

"It's four ingredients."

"Well, I like it. It's nice not to have to cook, for once."

Thing was, even if he was only pretending to enjoy it, that was more than most people had ever done for me. Hiding the truth to spare my feelings.

He poured us both another glass of

wine, and I couldn't help eyeing mine off. I'd tried not to drink more than a couple glasses a week since Noah came into my life full time, but my son wasn't here tonight. Besides, it was so rare for me to have company. It felt rude to refuse.

Almost the instant we both finished eating, Braden stood and began picking up plates.

"Hey," I said, a lame protest.

"I got this, big guy."

"No, you're my guest." I flinched for a second as my wounded arm gave off one of its annoying little hot twinges. I didn't quite manage to mask my reaction, and there was no doubt Braden noticed it.

Fucking wolf senses.

"See? Even your arm insists I should wash up."

It was tough to let him take over like

that. Pride still had a strong hold over me most times, but cooking had been hard enough with only one hand. The amount and kind of dishes I'd dirtied were pretty much impossible.

"Thanks, man," I said. Even that felt odd, since I rarely call people anything but their given names. Or some title. A pet name was really off kilter for me.

Wait.

Not a *pet* name.

What the fuck was I doing here?

A *nickname*.

Like between buddies.

I shook my head to try and clear it. All it seemed to do was filter the confusion down into my soul. Somehow it didn't really feel like confusion, though.

More like... friendship.

And was there really anything wrong

with being friends with Braden?

I followed him into the kitchen and grabbed a dishtowel.

"Uh-uh," he said, shaking his head. "I got this, I told you. Stay and chat, sure, but don't you lift a finger." He turned and winked. "And don't think for a second I don't know this is bugging the hell out of you, dude."

Finally, I relented, and I sat on the edge of the kitchen table and watched him work. My wolf raised his hackles out of uncertainty. Whether as a man or a beast, I'd always had the same instant reaction to an unfamiliar feeling.

Hackles up, teeth bared and growling. Attack before any shit hits my particular fan. My wolf paced inside me, trying to help me make sense of what this feeling was.

When Braden finished the dishes and turned to face me, it made me catch my breath. Realization hit me like a damn bear shifter.

I was attracted to the guy.

As if in protest at the truth, my damaged arm stung me again, and that time so sharply that I grunted with the pain.

Braden came straight across, his handsome face creased with concern, and he took hold of my upper arm and elbow. Tingles ran through my entire body, and rained down on my wolf.

"What do you need, Marius?"

"A fucking miracle."

He looked up at me, gliding his hand gently over the mangled skin of my stump. He slid the other hand down and pressed both his thumbs up against the old wound, gently at first. Then, he ground at the area like he was giving it a massage.

When it was clear he wasn't hurting me, he lifted the arm and took a much closer look at it.

He stroked his fingers over the damaged flesh, his face reflecting some mix of sadness and admiration.

It was the first time anybody had paid any kind of attention to the injury since the doctors did. Outside of stares and sneers by strangers, at least. Everyone who encountered me seemed to feel either revulsion or pity.

But my wolf could tell Braden, true to form, had nothing but empathy. The sadness was genuinely on my behalf, not from imagining the same injury on his own body.

And then, to my surprise, he kissed it. He pressed his mouth to my scarred and ugly flesh as if it was just a normal thing.

The wolf deep inside me whined, and pure need flooded through me. I couldn't remember the last time I'd had any kind of closeness with another being, apart from my son. And Noah still wasn't completely open with me.

Even though shifters are capable of secrets, it took a lot more effort. Too many senses in play. That was how I knew Braden was being as open with me as anybody ever had.

Without either of us speaking a word, I could taste his honesty.

Fuck, I could just about taste his heart.

And a moment later, when I grabbed him around the back of the neck and pulled him to me, I could taste his lips.

The guy responded immediately, opening up to me and drawing my tongue inside. He speared his fingers up into my hair and held on, his moans shifting into whimpers and then to growls.

Just like mine.

Every hair on my body bristled with pure desire.

To be held, to be touched.

To be *wanted,* not needed.

My wolf howled, and the sound came up through my body. I sang that note into Braden's hot mouth, and his wolf joined in as well. All the aggression I'd kept suppressed, just to help me fit in as a member of this new community, and as a father as well... it all came bubbling up.

I bit down on Braden's tongue, hard enough to hurt him. Hard enough that I drew blood. It didn't slow him down one bit. If anything, it just drove him harder.

Kellie had been wolf, too, but she'd never responded to me like that. Fuck, maybe I'd never responded to her the way I was to Braden. It was too hard to remember myself clearly from back then.

The only certainty in my body right then was that I wanted this man. In the most base and carnal ways. After a lifetime of obliviousness and assumptions about myself, it was all too much, and I shoved Braden away.

He stumbled back, his eyes quivering, caught somewhere between man and wolf. Fear overtook me like a tornado, but it wasn't fear for myself. I couldn't be sure I wouldn't hurt this man in some way.

I had a history, for fuck's sake.

Before Braden even spoke, I turned

and fled. Straight out the front door of my apartment, and on down toward the thickest part of the forest.

The shift overtook me before I reached the halfway mark. My limbs prickled and my bones creaked. Fur erupted from the skin of my arms and spread over my face. I hadn't shifted once since my injury, but the sensations were still so fucking clear.

I shed my clothing as best I could without breaking stride. Anything still on me just tore or dropped away. By the time I reached the tree line, I was fully shifted.

And I landed flat on my fucking snout, thanks to my missing front leg.

All that did was slice into my rage, which stemmed straight from my confusion and embarrassment anyway.

I scrabbled up onto my paws again and loped into the forest, learning quickly how to balance myself on only three feet.

This part of the forest was new to me, but it wasn't too far different from what I knew up on Stoke Ridge. The trees were the same, the birdsong, too. But the ground was smoother, which I welcomed.

The scents and sounds of the place embraced me like an old friend. Only by shifting this time did I realize how much I'd missed being wolf. How hard I'd been working to stop myself from doing it, for the sake of my son.

Once again, I knew I had Braden to thank for that. He awoke something ancient inside me. Not just my wolf, but my instincts.

And I'd turned away from him. Ran like he was the bear who took my arm. Simply because I was confused, and confusion made me a scared little kid.

Or at least, that confusion was the fuse that ignited the tightly bound powder keg inside me. The shitstorm of life that had rained down on me over the past couple of years.

I should have been strong enough to handle it all, but I suddenly realized all I'd done was to push it down, compress it. Wall myself off from every other fucker in the world. Even, to a certain degree, my son.

And then Braden came along, and with what looked like no effort at all, he simply scaled that fucking wall. Or more like he found a door.

And he opened me the fuck up.

Since my son lost his mother and came to me, I'd done everything required of me, and hopefully, a little more above and beyond. I'd provided, and I'd cared, and protected.

But who'd been there for me?

The short answer was Braden.

Only Braden.

And tonight he'd been there for me again, in a way I hadn't ever expected any man to be.

CHAPTER NINE

Braden

AS MARIUS TOOK flight away from me, I cursed myself.

Too much.

Too fast.

Everything I'd suspected about the man, everything my wolf had sensed, turned out to be true. Including the fragile and confused nature of his attraction to me.

As soon as I'd pushed my emerging wolf back down, I hurried out to follow him. The last thing I wanted was to leave him to process such a huge shift—no pun intended—on his own. Whether as man or wolf.

I'd barely taken a dozen steps before I found his shredded shirt, and realized he actually *had* shifted. I wasn't surprised. It was the way many of us dealt with a complex or challenging situation.

My best chance of finding him, and easing his turmoil, was to follow suit. I closed my eyes and let the tingling heat wash over me. The sweet pain and harsh sounds of bones breaking and reforming, the stretching and swelling of my jaw into a snout, the ragged tearing of fabric as arms and hands morphed into fur-covered paws.

Once I was wolf, I ripped away whatever clothing was left, and bounded into the forest, following the scent of that beautiful but troubled man.

Even with only three legs, he'd had a good head start and if not for my nose, I would have had no chance to follow. But I was so attuned to Marius that I could just about *see* his scent, even with all the other smells of the forest arguing for attention.

In mere minutes, I found him in Burton's Clearing, standing by the stream. He was facing me, all coiled up and ready for fight or flight. Even with his one front paw planted beneath his head to balance him, he was formidable.

Just like when he was human, he was ruggedly beautiful, and so damn huge. I paused for a moment at the edge of the clearing, crouching to keep my head low.

On the surface, it was an act of submission. In reality, it was more about reminding him that I was no threat to him. Not in any way.

He slackened his stance enough to give me hope, and I took a few cautious steps forward. The low growl he let rumble from his lips was clearly not a true warning. More a way to tell me to slow the hell down.

I licked my muzzle and let my tail swing lightly. Every step I took, he watched like I was prey. In under a minute, I was right there with him. I ducked my head under his and nudged forward, leaving the back of my neck open to him.

Marius huffed and leaned his head on

my back. He was so big, and so heavy, but it felt better than heaven to have him accept me like that.

His damaged leg was right before me, and this time, I gave it a quick lick. The wolf equivalent of kissing it, the way I did it just before, when we were human.

Marius made another huffing sound and dug his fangs into the skin of my back. I felt no threat from him. If anything, all it felt like was a connection. A show of possessiveness. As if he was grabbing hold of me, to stop me from getting away.

If only he knew just how crazy into him I was. The biggest trouble with being in wolf form was the narrow corridors of communication. Using scents, sounds, and body language was all well and good for the basics. Emotional state, territorial boundaries, even hunting tactics.

There were nuances to it all, and sometimes the absence of words made it purer and more meaningful. But wolf Marius was new to me. Not from the same clan. It was so easy to get signals wrong, especially with a shifter who was so out of touch with his inner beast.

But to try and tell Marius how I felt about him, I'd need the advantages of human speech. To help him work through the complicated nature of whatever he was going through, I'd need words, and so would he.

I stepped away from him and once again closed my eyes, letting the shift overtake me. In moments, I was back in human form, and I stood slowly, keeping my hands held out from my sides. I was not a threat to him and I wanted to make sure that fact made it through the wolf's consciousness to the man underneath.

Holy hell.

Even as wolf, Marius still reached up almost to my chest. With his head raised, his breath washed all the way up to my neck.

He watched my hands as I reached out toward him, and when I threaded my fingers into his thick fur, his skin quivered at the touch.

I was anything but certain about that moment, and where he'd go from there, emotionally. Physically. But he closed his eyes and huffed out a hot breath against my chest.

I snaked my fingers up and scratched behind his ears, moving myself forward and to my right, so he could lean on me a little more. To counterbalance for his missing leg.

Marius angled forward, pressing the top of his head to my belly. His breath was now coursing downward, and flowing over my cock. This big wolf could obviously pick up my scent, since his nose was only inches from my stiffening member.

We both stood frozen for a moment. Then the coarse fur in my hands gradually shrank away, as this brutish wolf shifted back into the delicious, huge man I'd first met.

Marius jumped instantly to his feet, towering over me. For one brief instant, the wild wolf remained still there behind his eyes, before he coiled his hand around the back of my neck and pulled me forward.

The impact of his mouth against mine

was as brutal and as painful as it was beautiful. I tasted blood and couldn't tell whose it was.

Probably both of ours.

Marius drove his tongue inside me and I gripped his hair, and stroked his scalp, just as I'd done when he was wolf. He growled deep into my throat like he still hadn't quite shifted all the way back.

I absolutely leaned hard into the kiss, doing all I could to own the moment. Marius made a tight fist in my hair, and stroked his damaged arm up and down my side.

I slid one hand down and caressed that arm, gliding around to the scarred end of it, and dragging my palm over the rough skin. Almost like I was stroking a massive cock.

Then, I eased my other hand out of his

hair and scratched down over the thatch of blonde curls on his chest, flicking a fingernail over his pebbled nipple. Then on down through the thick bush below his belly.

The instant my fingers met the skin of his cock, I whimpered, overwhelmed by his heat, his hardness, and his pure fucking size. I snaked my fist around him and squeezed tight, and Marius threw his head back with a deep, groaning howl.

"Christ, you're fucking beautiful," I moaned as I fell to my knees in worship. I buried my face in the curls of his bush, and drew in the musky scent of him. My wolf and human merged for a moment as both halves wrestled for dominance. For possession of this man's scent.

I stroked him, squeezing hard as I licked at his hip. Marius rested his big paw on the top of my head and let out a deep, breathy moan, and I lost a little bit more of my sanity.

As I drifted back inward, I hauled his huge thick cock downward. I glanced my lips across the shaft of him and once again soaked up the crazy heat of this man.

I stroked the long length of his gorgeous cock with my tongue, up one side and back down the other. I squeezed the fat blunt head in my hand as I dragged the face of my tongue slowly up the belly of his thick beast.

Marius tightened his grip on my hair, pulling hard enough to hurt me—just how I needed it. Desperation overtook me and I slid my fist back down his length and hauled his cock into my mouth, humming my appreciation as the flavor of him burst across my tongue from the pearl that had formed at his slit.

This immense, sexy beast of a man huffed out a deep-throated grunt that sounded as much like surprise as pleasure. His weighty cock filled my mouth so fucking beautifully it was like destiny.

The natural salty taste of him, seasoned by traces of his wolf, seemed to hook into my mind, and my soul. I drove myself forward and back, groaning with the pure bliss of pleasuring him. Showing him a tenderness that I felt certain he hadn't known for many, many years.

Maybe not ever.

Marius pumped his hips and drove himself deeper inside my mouth. He nudged at the back of my throat and I relaxed myself to give over control to him.

If there was one thing I was sure of, it was that control was exactly what he needed right at that moment.

Then, he released a long breath, sliced through clenched teeth, as his legs quivered, and his belly tightened. He groaned with pleasure and released my hair from his iron grip.

I glided him in and out, growling from pure hunger as I drew him closer and closer to his inevitable climax.

Marius leaned his good hand on my shoulder, and his whole body trembled. Then, he swore like he truly meant it, and a moment later, he flooded my mouth with his musky fluid.

Bursts of heat washed over my tongue, and I drank him down without a second's hesitation. His flavor filled my senses, all masculine and beastly.

The essence of nature and of life.

His last drops trickled out, and I let his hot, swollen length glide free of my mouth. Still kneeling, still gazing up at him, I stroked my hands up and down his tree trunk thighs, coarse hair tickling at my palms.

Marius seemed unable to look at me, though it was impossible to tell if he was ashamed, regretful, or overwhelmed. That was a moment of pure fucking perfection to me, but I knew he had to process it in his own way.

Still, he didn't resist, or pull away, when I pressed my mouth to his lower belly. Or when I gradually stood, licking the salt from his skin as I rose to my feet.

And even more promising, he didn't turn away as I tilted my head and kissed him again.

CHAPTER TEN

Marius

WHAT THE HELL just happened?

I mean, of course I knew.

But how the fuck had I lived this long and never understood myself?

Never realized what it was I was missing.

Braden's mouth worked around mine, his lips soft but his stubble harsh. My own flavor flooded my senses as he danced his tongue inside my mouth, running the appendage over my tongue and behind my teeth.

I took hold of his short, lush hair and dragged on it, harder than I'd meant to, but he just moaned with pleasure. When I wrapped my damaged arm around him, he leaned back into my embrace, baring his throat, his soft underbelly, to me.

More importantly, he put his trust in the strength of my biggest weakness, and despite everything else we'd just shared, that one moment made my heart soar like nothing ever had.

I was lost to this man. He was all I could think about, all I could see, the only scent I could find.

Until something new washed over me.

Bear.

My heart jolted with adrenaline as I raised my head, standing Braden back up on his feet.

Somewhere near.

Bear shifter.

Fuck.

Braden clearly sensed it as well. "What the fuck is a bear shifter doing in Burton's Clearing? Or anywhere in Gray Vale?"

Realization must have hit him at that moment. Either that, or he sensed my own turmoil. He pushed on my chest, hard enough to get me stepping backward.

"Come on, Marius. Don't even think about it, please."

Even though he knew the story of my mangled arm, that didn't mean he understood what I was thinking. Maybe he guessed I wanted some kind of vengeance, or that I simply wanted to see if it was the same guy.

Honestly, I had no idea what I was thinking, either. Just that a tornado of troublesome feelings had suddenly blown into my mind and were in danger of laying waste to the incredible warm sensations that Braden had awoken within me.

"Marius," he said, in a low, quiet voice that reached me through the funk of bear shifter, better than a roar would have. "Come home with me."

The undiluted need in Braden's voice cut through the danger, and the last of my lingering doubts.

With him was exactly where I wanted to be.

And somehow, the word *home* had never seemed more fitting.

"Let's go," I said, the words barely audible to human ears.

Braden reached up and tugged on my hair, and took my mouth in a far too brief kiss. That one touch eased the last of my tension and I kissed him back. Then, he eased out of my embrace and started running away toward the town, slowing down only long enough to shift back into wolf form. For speed, no doubt.

I couldn't say I blamed him. Having finally uncovered who I truly was, I needed to explore it fully.

As soon as fucking possible.

Still out of practice, it took me a moment longer to shift. But even on only three legs, I caught up with Braden again by the time we crested the tree line. I couldn't remember ever feeling so free, so light-hearted, and I took a playful nip at my man's hindquarters.

Fuck.

My man.

How the fuck did I so instantly come to think of him that way?

Even weirder, how the fuck did it feel like the absolute truth?

Outside his place, we shifted back. I wondered for a moment how we'd get in, since he had nowhere to keep any keys. But his door simply opened when he turned the handle, which was a sweet reminder of the trusting life here in Gray Vale.

Once inside, Braden turned and closed the door behind him. Then, he did the unthinkable and actually locked it.

I could wait no longer, and I gripped him around the throat, pushing him back against it. He closed his eyes and parted his lips, and the only thing I could do was dash my mouth against his, like the ocean slamming into the shore.

He hummed with a beautiful blend of relief and need as I plundered his sweet mouth. He fisted my hair with one hand and reached down for my cock with the other.

I switched hands, slamming my damaged forearm against Braden's chest to snare him against the door as I took his hot, hard cock in my one good hand.

He hissed as I tightened my fist around his shaft, and he growled as I stroked him, his beautiful voice growing harsher and more beastly with every fierce pump of my hand.

Braden slipped his mouth free of mine and pulled me down into the crook of his neck. His scent filled my head as his flesh filled my mouth. I sank my teeth into his skin as he clambered up onto me, throwing his legs around my waist and wrapping his arms around my neck.

"End of the hall. On the right."

My eyes spun as I tried to work out what he meant. My wolf was too close to the surface and he clouded my understanding.

But I spun on the spot and marched to where Braden indicated, finding his bedroom and snarling with a fresh burst of hunger for this man as I cleared the doorway.

We fell in a solid tangle of limbs and mouths, Braden's hot, firm body feeling utterly perfect beneath me. My cock ground against his, and they hooked together as we devoured each other's mouth in a ravenous kiss.

I had to make him feel as magical as he made me feel. Give him the pleasure he deserved. I hungered for this man in so many ways, and one of them absolutely required me taking him into my mouth.

It was too urgent to even work up to it. No more foreplay or teasing. I simply took my mouth off his and slid down his tight, hard body.

I kissed his rippled sack for a moment and drew in the deep woody essence of him. The blast of pheromones and musky sweat made me hunger for him even more than I already had been.

I slipped my hand behind his hard length and raised it so I could glide the face of my tongue right up the underside. He moaned so sweetly it just made me wilder.

Up and down I licked him, wetting

every fucking inch of his perfect cock. He fired his hands down into my thick hair and held on, tightening his grip when I flicked his head, loosening when I slid down to his balls.

Finally, I could wait no longer and I lifted his cock upright, and plunged my mouth down his length. All the fucking way down, surprising myself as much as Braden.

"Fuck," he moaned, gripping my hair so tightly it set my scalp on fire. I pumped up and down, soaking up the music of his moans as much as the symphony of his scents.

"Please, Marius..."

I glanced up at him, and the sweet, glistening need in his eyes made me weak for him. His wolf was so close to the surface, as was mine, and together they let me understand exactly what this man needed.

I slipped up off the end of him and raised one eyebrow. "Are you sure?"

"I need you, big guy. Please, fuck me."

"Jesus…" It came out as all breath and no voice.

Braden rolled over and reached to his bedside cabinet. He came back with a tube and popped the lid. He squeezed a load of clear gel out into his palm and reached toward me. When he touched my cock, I swore the bitterly cold lube turned to steam against my scorching skin.

Braden coated me, stroking up and down gently at first before tightening, and speeding up.

"Fuck," I whispered, almost losing myself in the intense pleasure. Then suddenly, he stopped, and rolled over, propping his smooth, perfect ass in the air.

"I fucking need you, Marius."

Nobody had ever sounded like that with me. So into the moment, so desperate to have me inside them.

Only now did I realize that the few women I'd been with had all been low level terrified. Even though they'd all been wolf, I must just have radiated such a violent energy.

I'd never once raised a hand to a lover. Not in anger or defense. Still, they'd all quivered and submitted as if I'd been about to snap at any moment.

There was such a level of trust between Braden and me that it made my cock pulse and grow inconceivably harder. Thicker.

"Jesus, you're beautiful," I growled

out, the words barely passing through my mind before gushing through my lips. I pressed my one good hand into the small of Braden's back and he arched a little deeper, opening his tight little ass up a little more.

I moved in close behind him, stroking my hand down his body until I could grip my own cock. Braden gripped his cheeks and pulled them apart, and I nudged myself home against his pretty, puckered hole.

"Yesss..." His need had transcended words and actions. It was an actual scent in the air, and my wolf took turns snarling and howling and rubbing against my skin. Licking his lips and crouching, ready for action.

The kiss of his ass hole against my tip sent a sharp, sensual thud through my body, like an electric shock. It took all my will power to keep from punching forward. Maybe Braden would be okay with it, but I knew my own size and power. And I already cared too much about this man to risk hurting him like that.

"Do it, Marius. Fuck me. As hard as you like."

"Fuck..."

I lost it at that moment. Beast and man merged inside me, and I thrust hard, driving half my thickness into Braden's tight, blistering hot ass. He threw his head back and let out a long moan that moved closer and closer to a howl with every passing second.

Harder, faster, deeper, I thrust myself into him, driving farther inside until the blissful moment I was completely connected. That instant when the hardness of my hips slammed against the smooth heat of his ass. My whole long, steely cock was inside him, and I was fucking *home*.

Braden grunted with pain and pleasure, and arched his back like a drawn bow. I rested my damaged arm on his lower back and threw my good hand around his throat from behind.

With every hard, ragged thrust of my hips, I squeezed tight around Braden's neck. He whimpered with undiluted need, bouncing himself back at me, drawing more pleasure from inside my core than I could ever have imagined.

This beautiful man writhed before me, tightened around me. The sharpness I felt on first contact had doubled.

Tripled.

My wolf snarled inside me, as I

instinctively knew somehow that Braden's did the same within him.

As my climax crouched and readied to pounce, my teeth lengthened, my nails grew into claws. Braden's skin rippled as his muscles danced beneath it. His whole body darkened as the hint of a shift overtook him, and his fur threatened to appear.

And then I swore I was struck by lightning.

My orgasm hit me with all the power of a shift, and all the sharpness of a blade. I clawed my hand, and the scent of blood coursed its way into my head. The hunger of a predator bit heartily into my very human ball of bliss, taking my climax to a level that I'd never known could exist.

I unleashed bolts of heat deep inside Braden, punching against him like a sledgehammer as the most intense release flowed through me. This went beyond just the physical.

This was an affirmation of my own life.

My being.

My entire self.

Braden howled in harmony with me, a dark wall of sound that would reach every fucking inch of this town. Even human ears could hear us as we claimed each other.

When my climax finally eased, my wolf panted as hard as I did, and together we softened and released our hold on this incredible man.

I glided out of Braden, and he swung right around and dived at me, mashing his lips into mine, and falling back, hauling me down on top of him.

We landed with a thud, our kisses

turning slower but deeper. His breath, his heat, his scent merged with mine until it was impossible to separate one man from the other.

"That was incredible, Marius."

"I've never... known it could be like that."

His handsome face lit up with a smile, and held my head in his two good hands. He gave me one last light kiss and then rolled over and backed into me. He pulled my mangled arm over him like a blanket and nestled in against my body.

Like *he* was home.

CHAPTER ELEVEN

Braden

I CAME AWAKE gradually, to the feeling of hot breath washing over the back of my neck. Marius's thick arm was still draped over me, his hard body still nestled in behind me. As if we hadn't moved at all through the night.

The morning light was just beginning to beat away the darkness of night, and I soaked up that moment of quiet bliss as the luminous beams split the curtains.

Who knew what the day had in store?

I had never slept better, deeper, or longer than I did in the arms of this big, damaged man. His heat, his size, and his aura conspired to make me feel safer than I ever had. Something I'd never known was even missing from my life.

Marius stirred, and I slowly spun to face him. I honestly didn't know how he'd feel, in the light of day, after the night we had. There was plenty of chance he'd regret the whole thing. Not just because he'd never been with a man before, but because I was his son's teacher.

So many layers.

When he opened his beautiful crystal blue eyes, though, he opened my heart as well. The smile on his rugged face told me everything I needed to know.

I leaned over and slanted my mouth over his, and thankfully, he kissed me back. Deeply. It was too soon to believe any kind of fairytale, but that kiss, and the connection between us, slammed into me at a level way deeper than just the physical.

My wolf and his were in harmony. Marius felt the same way I did. I didn't need to ask him anything to know that. Everything I felt in my heart was also drifting through the air between us, as a rich range of scents.

As our kiss deepened, Marius growled with need. His thick, hard cock pressed into my thigh, and holy fuck but I wanted him again.

Immediately.

The big brute rolled me onto my back

and bumped my legs apart with his knee. I spread them willingly, begging him to do to me whatever the fuck he wanted.

He held himself up on his battered arm, and reached down to squeeze my cock, all the while plunging his tongue into my mouth. But where last night had been savage and harsh, this morning his kisses were like the tide.

Slower, smoother, but utterly relentless.

I threw my arms around his neck and held him to me, returning his passion with a hunger I'd never felt with any other lover.

Marius released his grip on my hardness and came down, resting his entire wonderful weight on top of me. Holding me down as if I'd ever try to escape his embrace.

He ground his wonderful, swollen cock against mine and sent deep, subterranean shocks of pleasure running through my body.

Even though every move he made was softer, slower than it had been last night, it was the same as his kiss.

Deeper.

More intense.

This time, it meant something more to him than just scratching an itch he'd never known was there.

He knew, I knew, and our wolves knew... this time it meant everything.

I broke our kiss for only long enough to reach over for the lube. I had him greased up in seconds, and even on only one arm, he held himself up easily. Towering over me in the most delicious way.

He rested his injured arm against my chest as I notched his thick cock in place. I pulled my legs right up to my chest and made myself as open to him physically as I already was emotionally.

Marius let loose with a low, rumbling moan, then drove himself deep into me. The sweet, stretching pain of the invasion was beyond perfect. Everything about this man made me whole.

"Fuck…" he snarled. "You feel so fucking good, Braden."

I couldn't talk. I could barely breathe as he glided in and out, slower and more measured than I expected. Last night was raw and ravenous, and such an incredible release. It had been a wonderful, gluttonous night of hedonism.

This morning, Marius seemed more like a connoisseur. Savoring every moment, every sensation. His eyes never left mine, and he watched intensely as every thrust of his magnificent cock played itself out through my body and across my face.

His gaze sliced through me, cutting so deep I swore he was opening me up, down to my soul. Letting out the wolf within. Taking me back to my most elemental form, and meeting me there the same way, through the connection we shared.

The way he rocked against me, driving in and out, went beyond pleasure and into some new realm I'd never imagined. I threw my hands around the back of his neck and hauled him down, desperate for his mouth.

Marius opened up and plundered me, with tongue and cock, as if drinking my essence. We formed a circle, connected top and bottom, and my heart soared as much as my cock did.

When Marius sat up, I held on so tight that he hauled me up with him. I straddled his lap, still riding his thick cock, still drinking from his sweet mouth.

He kept his hurt arm as far around me as he could, and reached his good hand down, gripping my cock and squeezing so tight. He stroked me hard and fast as he punched his hips up at me.

My wolf and his both paced in circles, snarling at their cages of bone and flesh. Desperate to come out and take their share of sensations.

Marius leaned back, his mighty fist pounding my cock into sweet oblivion as he took his own pleasure from my ass.

My whole body ignited with electrical prickling, as if I was about to be struck by lightning, as the head of his cock brushed over my prostate and I clamped my muscles around him.

Marius's growls became grunts, became ragged breaths, as he surfed the same wave of pleasure I did.

Then, I swore I truly had been electrocuted as my climax hit me. It came at me as if from outside my body, in a rush, like a pack of wolves sinking their fangs into my flesh all at once.

Marius shot his heat deep inside me, searing my walls as I pumped mine out over our chests and bellies.

The pleasure hit me, harder than pain and hotter than fire. It radiated through me, centered bizarrely on the side of my neck.

For a few seconds—that felt like hours—of bliss, I rocked my hips forward and back, letting my body drink in the majesty of Marius.

Only when the haze of climax cleared, did I finally come back to my senses. To find I had this big, wonderful man's teeth embedded in my flesh.

Right at the side of my neck.

***

We held still for a short while longer, before we both realized exactly what had just happened. Not just that we'd made the most incredible love I'd ever experienced. But Marius had given me his mark. Claimed me.

As we came apart, it was clear he was as surprised as I was. His rugged face somehow looked boyish. Confused, yet beneath that, deeply understanding of exactly what he'd done.

"I, uh…"

He shook his head, but not in denial. Just to clear it. Already our bond had grown well enough that I could sense his emotions and thoughts more clearly than before.

"It's okay, Marius."

"But I… we didn't talk about it. We've hardly even…"

He backed away a little. Distancing himself from the moment as much as from me. Giving himself space to think.

Well, fuck that.

I didn't need time or space. I already knew how I felt. About him, about us, even about Noah. This little pack of three was the family I'd longed for. And I would do anything to be the home that Marius needed.

I crawled toward him and he watched

my every move. That prickly exterior he'd worn since the moment he'd arrived in Gray Vale, that he'd only let slip when we were together... it was coming back.

His natural reaction to confusion.

The instant I touched my lips to his, he calmed. He sighed, and opened up to me, and I eased him onto his back.

"I promise, Marius. It's okay. It's more than okay."

I picked up his hand and pressed his fingers to the still raw wound on my neck. His touch awoke the same kind of pleasurable agony that his cock did in my ass, and I sighed as fresh tingles poured through my blood.

"It's perfect," I whispered.

When he spoke, it was barely audible, even to wolf ears. But now that we were mated, it didn't need to be.

"I wasn't even thinking. It was pure instinct."

"It was the right instinct. Can't you feel it?"

He said nothing, but he stroked that mark he gave me and made a low humming sound.

My belly interrupted the moment by loudly growling.

Marius finally cracked a smile, and sat up. "You got a wolf in your belly, or you just hungry?"

"A little of both. Plus, don't forget horny."

He put his huge paw in my face and pushed me down onto my back. "Little whore," he said with a chuckle. "No time for that. I have to go and pick Noah up this morning."

My belly tightened in anticipation of

the question I had to ask. "You want me to... uh... come with?"

I knew the answer would be no before he said it. Maybe before he even knew. But the fact he had to think about it was, to me, a victory. A week ago it would have been an immediate and automatic rejection.

"Might be a little too confronting," Marius said. "For Noah."

I nodded in understanding. Understanding that Noah likely wasn't the one who'd feel confronted, but also that Marius would still need time to adjust to this.

"Well," I said. "I need a shower. Someone made a damn mess of me."

That at least brought a smile. "I take it you have food in your kitchen?"

"Pretty sure. Maybe even enough for a

big lug like you. Help yourself, man."

"If you're lucky I might just whip something up for you." He shoved me back down again, with a broad grin covering his features. "But don't count on it."

I made sure to take a little extra time in the shower to let the water ease the wonderful aches and pains of the previous night. The rapid shifting and running, and of course, the incredible sex. Oh, and the even more intense morning fuck, as well.

All cleaned up and warmed up, I threw a towel around my waist and headed out to the kitchen.

And stopped short in my tracks, confronted by the sight of Noah standing there, gazing at me. Confused, surprised. But I couldn't help noticing the little flash of genuine pleasure in his eyes at seeing me, either.

I opened and shut my mouth a couple times as I tried to work out what the hell was going on.

Why on earth was Noah here?

He was still supposed to be at his sleepover.

"Good morning, Braden."

I glanced at the front door, where Pauline herself was standing, just about to leave.

Pauline, the mom of Vincent.

The boy Noah had a sleepover with.

One of *my* moms.

"Oh, uh... hey, Pauline."

"I came here to ask if you knew Marius's address, since Noah couldn't remember it." She kinked one eyebrow upward. "Imagine my surprise when I found the man himself here."

Fuck.

This was gonna be awkward. Not for me, exactly. I mean, I'm out as out can be and there are very few people who don't know that.

But for Marius?

Fuck, this whole situation had come out of nowhere. The guy hadn't had a moment to steel himself in private for acceptance, let alone in public.

I glanced across at the big man, who was pale and evasive. And I improvised the first lie I could think of.

"So, uh... thanks for trying to fix my sink, buddy. I guess I'll have to call a plumber."

"Uh..." Marius straightened a little. "No problem. I was glad to... lend a hand."

One glance across at Pauline told me

she wasn't buying it. Not even close. But that wasn't really my concern.

"Well," she said, cocking an eyebrow. Her gaze wandered just south of my eyes, and I realized she must be looking at my neck. At the mark Marius had given me. "I'll leave you guys to it."

"Wait," I blurted. "Just let me get dressed and I'll walk with you."

"Guys, it's fine," Pauline said, her mouth curling up at the corners.

"No, I wanted to discuss... uh... Vincent's progress."

Which was absolute bullshit, of course, but I had to speak to her away from Noah. At least my bullshit worked, as I knew it would. No mom could resist talking about their own kids.

Once I was dressed, I strolled back out to the kitchen. I told Marius to make himself at home, making sure I said it loudly enough for Pauline to hear. I ruffled Noah's hair with a smile, which he thankfully returned, and then headed out the door.

I made sure Pauline and I were a good distance from my place before I sucked in a breath to speak. She managed to get in just before me.

"Braden Craig, you devil."

"Huh?"

"Oh, come on, now. It doesn't take a genius to work out what's going on."

Okay, so that confirmed that she was not even slightly fooled.

"Okay... Pauline, I know what it looks like, but—"

"Hey, it isn't really my business, y'know? I mean, I'm pissed, of course, because it's completely unfair."

"Hey, I treat all my students the same."

"What? Oh no, fuck that noise. I know you wouldn't let it change your teaching. It's just... I had visions of sinking *my* teeth into that big, rough hunk of a man."

It was my turn to give her the side-eye. She fired back with a smirk.

"What? Why the hell do you think I went out of my way to try and drop his boy home?" She sighed theatrically. "Oh, well. Another one bites the cock."

"Well, anyway," I said. "Obviously I'm not so bothered about... being discovered. It might be a little wrong given the whole teacher and parent situation, but I can wear that. It's Noah I'm worried about."

"You know Gray Vale has never been bothered about homosexuality. None of the kids will say anything."

"It's not even that. I don't think Noah

would have a problem with his father being gay."

If he truly is.

"But the kid's been through a shit-ton of stuff already. He lost his mom and hasn't recovered yet. I don't know that he's ready to accept me as anything more than his teacher."

Pauline nudged me with her elbow. "You'd make a great mom."

I laughed along with her, but it wasn't without worry. Because I knew I couldn't truly fill that mom-sized gap in Noah's life. But if I was lucky, I'd at least get the chance to be part of his pack.

CHAPTER TWELVE

Marius

WHEN PAULINE TURNED up with Noah, I lost the power of speech. Of thought. Everything I'd shared with Braden last night, and in the morning, suddenly felt like a betrayal.

And why?

I had nothing to feel guilty about. No partner to cheat on, nobody I'd made promises or pledges to. But I still hadn't wrapped my head around the massive shift in my perception of who I was, and suddenly I felt I was facing judgment from a relative stranger.

More importantly, the moment Noah saw me at his teacher's place, with Braden coming out of the bathroom wearing nothing but a towel, I could sense the confusion radiating off my son.

As lame as it was, Braden offered me up an excuse and I ran with it. But we were all fucking shifters in this town. There was no way Pauline didn't figure out exactly what happened. My only hope was that Noah believed the ridiculous half-assed story.

I mean, why the fuck was this woman even trying to take my son home?

The arrangement was I would pick

Noah up at ten. And now everything was fucked.

There was no way I could keep seeing Braden. Noah wasn't even ready for a new *woman* in his life.

How the hell was he meant to adjust to his father being with a man?

It was all so far out of my comfort zone I couldn't process it.

But holy fuck.

There was no denying the pull of that mark I gave Braden. I could feel him, even now. Across the distance, across time, whatever. I was in Braden's blood, now, and his blood was in me. And all because I lost my stupid fucking head while we made love.

It surprised me to realize that's what it had been.

Making love.

When we started last night, I thought we were just fucking. I tried to convince myself I was simply taking something that was offered, just for some kind of relief.

Braden blew that out of the water almost instantly with his passion, his empathy and his sheer voracious appetite. He opened up rooms in my head and in my heart that hadn't just been locked away.

They were fucking secret.

I hadn't even known I had such a deep well of emotion to draw on.

To feel with.

I had to at least discuss the situation with Noah, though. Once Braden and Pauline left, I wasn't entirely sure what to do. But remembering that the door was unlocked when we arrived last night, I figured it was fine to just leave it that way.

We headed out, and as I struggled to think up the words I needed to use, I put my hand on Noah's shoulder.

"Did you... have a good time last night, Noah?"

"It was fine." He walked beside me but made no attempt to get close to me, or hold my hand. "Why did Mister Craig leave like that?"

Was that a trick question?

Had he worked out what happened?

"Oh, he has stuff to do today." I didn't want to actively lie to my son, and I hoped that he didn't ask questions that would drag me down to those depths.

"It was nice to see him."

You don't know the half of it, son. "You like him, huh?"

Noah nodded, keeping his words to

himself like he used to back at the start. When we first got essentially forced together.

Every time I thought I'd made a little inroad with the kid, he shut himself off again. I got the feeling he'd sensed that hail-Mary lie that Braden tossed out there, and it bothered him.

All that did was reinforce it to me. He wasn't ready for me to move on with anyone, yet.

And the fucked up mixed messages that would come from me being with his classroom teacher?

That was out of the damn question.

***

My determination to end things with Braden lasted all of two hours. That was when he called me, and I swooped on my cell and answered it like I was a fucking teenage girl.

"Marius." That was all he said, but it had me closing my eyes in ecstasy. My tongue buzzed like I was touching it to a battery, from the connection between us. Where I'd lapped at his neck as I marked him.

"Hey," I replied, which was more than I thought I'd be able to come up with. There wasn't any way to put into words what I knew I had to say. That we had to stop, even as we'd barely started.

That no matter what, I had to protect Noah.

"Can we meet up?"

There was nothing I wanted more in the here and now than to see that man. To touch him. Explore whatever the hell it was going on between us, both at human and wolf level.

"I have Noah."

"I know. But there's the park. He can play and we can watch him while we talk."

The guy didn't have any kids of his own but he still seemed like a more organized parent than I ever would be. That feeling scared the fuck out of me more than anything. I could see myself diving head first into Braden. In truth, it was too late to think of doing anything else, now that I'd sunk my teeth into his beautiful neck.

"Okay. Sounds good." I wished I could say the same about myself. That I sounded good. In truth, I sounded like a fucking meathead.

We met up an hour later, and when he saw his teacher, Noah's little face lit up.

At least, by his standards. He smiled and held his head a little higher than usual.

"Hey, my man," Braden said, dropping to one knee and holding out his fist. This time around, my son landed his punch properly. With some real weight. It looked like something that had become a regular thing between the two of them.

"Hey, son," I said. "Why don't you go play on the swings? Braden and I have a couple things to talk about."

Noah looked from me to Braden as if needing permission from both of us. A moment later, he strolled over and stood off to the side of the other kids, probably waiting for them to invite him to play.

Braden sat on a bench and I took the seat beside him. "So, that was fucking unexpected this morning," he said. I wasn't really sure it was something we could make light of. Not yet, at least.

"She really caught me by surprise, man."

"It's all good. I've known Pauline a long time. You want us to be secret, she'll do her part. It's just..." He sighed and scratched his hand back through his hair. "I don't know how we'd even hope to keep everyone from knowing. There's, like, three people in the whole town who aren't wolf."

There it was. My chance to give this thing a mercy killing. "Braden..."

"Fuck," he hissed, clearly reading me like a picture book. "Don't do this to me, Marius. Please?"

"I have to, man. Noah's not ready for... other people."

"He's not? Or you're not?"

How could I explain it properly?

HIS WOUNDED WARRIOR

That my son not being ready, and me not, were two sides of the same coin.

Maybe that made me weak.

Maybe selfish.

Maybe—probably—a fucking coward.

"This is not how I want it to be, Braden. I want... fuck, I want you."

"Then have me. Take me." He grabbed my arm and pulled it upward, and I knew exactly why. He wanted me to touch my hand to the mark I left on him.

Only, he'd grabbed my damaged arm.

He didn't let that stop him. It was as if he meant to get that one. He simply leaned forward and pressed my roughened stump to his fresh and beautiful wound.

"You *know* what that mark means, dude."

Even through the muffling of scar

tissue, I still felt it.

Braden's heart pounding in time with mine.

My spine tingling as it searched for his.

My wolf leaning heavily against his.

Two sides of the same coin.

"Braden, please... I can't."

"You can. This isn't Stoke Ridge. We can be as open as you fucking like."

Christ, I wanted it like food.

Like air.

Braden could read that on me, of course, just as I could read it on him. But he could obviously sense my fear, and the reasons for it.

This beautiful man swallowed, his eyes reflecting mine. Both of us glistening with a raw emotion that I was too chickenshit to give a name to.

Because what if it was *love?*

This was so new. We'd met a few months back, and been in each other's company a couple weeks, but we'd only been *together* for one fucking night. One sweet, passionate night that I would remember for the rest of my life.

But that would be all I could take from it.

The memories.

"I'm sorry, Braden. I can't choose anyone else over Noah."

"You don't have to. I'm in for it. All of it."

"He's a scared little kid."

A flash of anger ignited in Braden's eyes. "I wonder where he gets that from."

The fire in his words cut me bone deep, and had my wolf crouching and snarling. "Watch it, man."

"Noah is far more resilient than you give him credit for, Marius."

That was the final straw. Nobody lectured me on my own fucking son. I lashed out with my good hand and snared Braden around the throat. The red mist and tingles of a shift hovered right around the edges, waiting for me to give in to it.

Instead, I squeezed, and Braden closed his eyes in what looked like bliss. Only after a moment did I realize I was pressing my fingers into the mark I gave him.

A fresh wave of panic hit me and I pulled my hand back like Braden was a snake, coiled and ready to strike. I stood and marched away, collecting Noah and heading for home.

Feeling more like a coward than I ever had. Emptier than I ever knew I could.

Because I left my heart back there on

that bench, with the man I loved.

CHAPTER THIRTEEN

Braden

THE NEXT COUPLE of days were a fucking living hell for me. Catching short glimpses of Marius only when he dropped Noah off at school or picked him up. Tiny moments of eye contact that made my mate mark throb with need.

There was no doubt Marius sensed it as well. The clench in his jaw, the heavy creasing of his brow, every time he saw me, confessed the depth of feeling in the man.

True to his usual form, he somehow managed to honor his word and keep his distance, despite the fact it was hurting him at least as much as it hurt me. To see each other mostly from across the classroom, to exchange only the occasional word in crisp, cool tones. And never anything personal between him and me. Only ever discussing Noah and his progress.

By the Thursday afternoon, I was a damn mess. Marius keeping aloof like that had me aching inside. I rolled through every day, every lesson, half in a trance, constantly distracted by the pulsing heat of my mate mark reaching out for my other half. My body crying for him. My wolf switching on a dime between whining and sulking, snarling and clawing at my skin.

Even through all that, I felt I'd been doing my job well, and keeping things on track. It was only when the students went for an outing on Friday afternoon that I knew something was up. When Kayleigh came in to my classroom as I cleaned up, ready for the next week.

"Braden. Got a moment?"

"For you? Always."

The kink of one eyebrow told me she was not in the mood for lame-ass charm. "Take a seat."

All the tension inside me from the situation with Marius threatened to harden into diamond. There was definitely something wrong, and it was clearly important. Just what I needed when I was barely keeping a lid on my pain and frustration.

Once I sat, Kayleigh crossed her arms and stared into me. She had the most intense focus I'd ever seen in a human. It made me wonder if she'd once been nipped by a shifter, just in passing. Not enough to make her become, just enough to give her heightened senses.

"I've had complaints," she said, not without some warmth in her voice. "Some of the parents think you're... playing favorites. With Noah."

"Let me guess. Pauline especially?"

"I'm not at liberty to say," she replied, but confirming my suspicion with a nod.

"She's just saying that because—"

"She's saying it because it's true, Braden." Kayleigh sighed and relaxed her body language, sitting on the edge of my desk. "Honey, I get it. I saw your neck the Monday after he marked you. Just because I don't literally feel what a mate mark does to you, doesn't mean I don't understand that it happens. That you gotta answer to your wolf just as much as to your human side."

Even without mentioning his name, she managed to bring me low. I leaned my elbows on my knees and closed my eyes.

"It doesn't take shifter senses to see how he's pulled away from you."

"He doesn't think Noah is ready. That's what he says."

"You don't agree?"

I stood and thrust my hands back through my hair in frustration. "I don't agree, no. It's Marius who's not ready. Except he only worked that out *after* he wrecked me for anyone else."

"Honey, what happened to the guy who's stayed friends with every ex he's ever had?"

I stopped short of howling in pain and frustration. "That's different. It was easy with them because none of them mattered like Marius does. As much as I thought they meant at the time, there was nothing between us that could touch what I have with Marius. What he *had* with me."

"Braden. Honey."

I could hear the words she hadn't yet said, as surely as if she really had said them. That I should give it time. That either he'd come around, or I'd get over him. But that was human thinking. That didn't take into account the depth and irrevocability of this fucking bite on my neck.

"I... I think I'm gonna have to leave

town."

"Honey, no."

"Not forever. I hope. But for a while. I don't see any other answer."

Kayleigh came forward and swept me into a hug. "I won't let you."

I leaned into her embrace, and rested my forehead on her shoulder. "Sorry, human girl. You don't have the strength to stop me."

"Maybe I don't, but the kids will. You can't turn away from them."

"The kids aren't here right now, Kayleigh. I can turn away from people who aren't here."

She tensed against me. "You're... not thinking of leaving right away? You can't."

"I have to. It's eating me up, inside and out, that I'm so close to the man and can't be with him. I need to at least put some distance between us."

I was closer than I'd ever been to swearing at work. Even though it was just Kayleigh and me, and it'd be okay, the teacher side of me still held the balance over the man. And the wolf.

"Braden, at least wait until they're back from Burton's Clearing in a couple hours. Would you give me that much?"

"Wait... they're at Burton's Clearing?"

"Of course. You didn't read the memo?"

Jesus.

The bear shifter.

What if he was still there?

"We have to get them back, Kayleigh."

Normally, she knew better than to argue with wolf senses, but this time it obviously seemed to come out of the blue. With all my talk of leaving, she probably thought I was simply off my damn rocker.

"What are you talking about, B?"

"We caught the scent of a bear shifter there. It wasn't just in passing. It was heavy, like the guy had been living there for weeks, or even longer."

"Holy hell. And you didn't say anything?"

I winced in reaction. "I meant to, but..."

In the moment I'd scented the guy back then, I'd had every intention of telling the authorities. I'd just gotten distracted by the majesty of Marius, and the intense, soul-searing sex we'd had.

My mind had obviously been running pretty much on empty since Marius pushed me away.

If I'd even so much as caught the memo about the school outing, I'd have mentioned it then. More proof how badly I'd dropped the ball in my messed up state.

Kayleigh pulled out her cell phone to make some calls.

"Can I?" I asked her, holding out my hand. "He won't pick up when I call from my phone."

She sighed and handed it over. "Be quick. We have to tell the guards."

I fired my finger at the screen, tapping out the numbers for Marius's phone.

"Marius Voss."

"Marius. It's Braden. Please listen."

Even through the phone I picked it up. Relief, concern, and something much deeper. I wouldn't risk giving that emotion a name. Not while he still had the power to eviscerate my soul a second time.

"What's wrong?"

"We have to get to Burton's Clearing."

"I don't know where that is."

"Where we smelled the bear shifter. Noah's there."

"What the fuck?"

"School outing. I didn't know."

He said nothing more. Just disconnected the call. I handed the phone back to Kayleigh and ran for the door. By the time I hit the outside, I'd stripped off completely, and a moment later I was wolf.

I'd never run so fast. Not even when I chased down Marius that first night. Greyhounds had nothing on me.

I hit the edge of the forest and steamed ahead along the paths, the trees and shrubs whipping past me in a blur. My only focus was Burton's Clearing.

The funk of bear hit me when I was

still a few hundred feet away. Then, the sound reached me. The fearful whimpering of children, the trembling false calm of adult voices alternately soothing their charges and reasoning with their foe.

And the snuffling, grumbling noises of a bear. It sounded irritated more than anything. Like it just wanted everyone to leave. Thank fuck for small mercies.

I stopped at the edge of the clearing, rather than bursting in and startling the big guy. He had to have known I was coming, of course. I'd made no effort to keep quiet.

Still, charging out of the scrub at breakneck speed could only have made things worse, so I made sure to slow down to a walk before making an entrance.

Immediately, I knew I'd made the right

decision. This guy was beyond big, even by bear standards. Even more than that, he was clearly wired on something. Standing on his back legs and towering over us all, he kept shaking his massive head, and blinking. Mouthing at nothing, pulling back his lips to bare his teeth at phantoms flying around him that only he could see. What teeth he had, anyway.

When he swung my way, he pawed at his mouth, even going so far as to draw blood from his own tongue.

Normally, we lived in a tense harmony with bear shifters. It wasn't like wolves and bears were natural enemies or anything, but we were competitors at the very least.

Even though I knew I stood a better chance of defending the kids and teachers when I was in wolf form, I had to take a chance. This situation needed the human touch.

I let my shift come on slowly, taking almost a minute to get back into human form, hoping to inspire the bear to do the same.

It seemed it was working, too. The bear's fur gradually paled and shrank, and he dropped to all fours as he began shrinking back to human size.

"Mister Craig!"

I didn't have to turn around to know it was Noah. A second later the boy slammed into me, his little arms gripping my leg like two tiny pythons.

Whatever this bear was on, it had him highly spooked. Noah's sudden cry and movement got the big guy all keyed up again, and he rose on his back legs and raised his head in panic as he fled back into his beastly shape.

I still thought maybe things could be okay. He'd been bear when I arrived, and hadn't done anything. A quick glance across at the kids and teachers told me they were all terrified, but ready to move.

I signaled with my eyes and a nod of my head for them to start making their way backward through the brush, and I waved my arms to keep big bear boy's attention on me.

"Noah," I murmured. "Can you go back with your classmates?"

"No. I want to stay with you."

"Please, son," I said, and suddenly I realized that was exactly how he felt to me. Like my own son. He was that important to me, and I'd been missing him almost as much as I'd been missing his father.

A moment later, it was all academic. The bear dropped to all fours and swayed his massive head side to side. He sprang forward, heading straight for us, just as Marius, in his massive wolf form, came charging into the clearing.

CHAPTER FOURTEEN

Marius

I'D NEVER KNOWN a rage like the one that overtook me as I burst into the clearing. The two people who meant more to me than life itself, facing down a motherfuckin' enormous bear.

As big as my wolf was, that furry black bastard dwarfed me. None of that mattered, though. I only had one duty and that was to throw myself in his path. Whatever shit he was planning, it was my responsibility to take it to protect my son.

And my mate.

I launched myself into the ever-narrowing gap, landing in front of Braden and Noah and facing the oncoming danger. I crouched as best I could on three legs, snarling like my life depended on it.

Because it very well might.

The bear cocked his head and—thank fuck—slowed to a stop only inches from me. I gathered my strength, bunching up on my hind legs, ready to pounce. This guy threatened my family. No way I was taking that lying down. I wouldn't stand a chance, wolf against bear, but the only thing I was certain of was that I was going down swinging.

"Marius."

Braden's voice behind me pulled my attention for a second.

Why the fuck was he still standing there?

Why hadn't he taken my son to safety with all the others?

I couldn't even spare a second to look back at him. Instead, I concentrated on our connection and begged him to get away while he could. While the bear was still confused by me challenging him.

"Marius," he said again, this time resting his hand on my back. "Please. Don't take him on. He's just... confused."

Confused?

If Braden wanted to see confused, he only had to look into my mind.

What the hell was he talking about?

A second later, I felt it. My mate

actually *was* looking inside me. Tingling tendrils of sensation coursed through my blood as Braden connected his thoughts with mine.

There were no words. It was just senses. Images, memories, emotions. Despite my instinct to stay wolf, to stand and fight—and die, without a doubt—Braden had some other idea in mind.

Could I truly listen to his advice?

His wishes?

I knew combat. Sometimes, I thought it was all I knew. In that moment, faced by an insurmountable threat, it was the only reaction that came to me.

"Daddy," Noah said. "Please, listen."

Every inch of my skin quivered in reaction. My son had never called me that before. It was always *dad*, or *father*, or he'd find some way not to call me anything at all.

The bear still hadn't moved off the place he'd stopped. Just swayed his head side to side, worked his gap-toothed mouth in weird ways. It was suddenly clear that something wasn't right with him. That was what Braden and Noah were trying to tell me. The guy wasn't angry, probably wasn't even vicious. Just fucking messed up.

I closed my eyes and welcomed the shift. Let it wash through me. Let it calm me, which had never happened from a shift before. There was no doubt in my head that Braden was the stabilizing factor for me.

Back in human form, I stood slowly, holding out my hand, palm forward, toward our big bear intruder. He leaned to the side and scratched at the side of his head with one paw, and it looked to me like he was chasing invisible insects.

I risked a glance back over my shoulder, and the sight of both my guys there, fit and uninjured, gave me strength. Braden reached through our mate connection to help keep me cool and balanced, and it was exactly what I needed.

"Hey, buddy," I said to the bear. "You seem to be outta place here."

He snuffled and jumped with just his front paws, like he was testing me. To see if I'd turn and run, see if I'd shift. Just see what was what, maybe.

"You wanna shift back, that'd be cool," I continued. "If not, that's cool, too."

He let out a low, rumbling noise, and I sent a message through to Braden to get my son out of the clearing. Thankfully, he was already way ahead of me on that, and had handed Noah over to one of the other teachers who'd come back for him.

I paused for a little while, until their footsteps faded and I knew they were likely all the way back out of the forest. Assuming I survived this, I'd pick Noah up later.

Thing was, I needed Braden to leave as well, but the damn fool stayed.

How the fuck was I supposed to protect him if he stayed in the danger zone?

My mate clearly picked up on my fears. He came over and put his hand on my shoulder, the way he'd touched my back when I was wolf. "You're not alone. You never have to be alone."

He also must have sensed the whirling dilemma inside me. How to best handle the danger when all I'd ever known was fight or flight. I was more grateful than ever when he stepped back to the edge of the clearing. Letting me work out what the fuck I had to do without having to worry about the man I loved.

I decided to just go with what amounted to common ground.

I raised my damaged arm and leaned slowly toward our big, brutish companion.

"Maybe you can see, I've had my run-ins with your kind before, brother." I didn't feel any real kind of fraternity with this guy, of course. But somehow it seemed to be the right way to address him. Show some solidarity. Make it so we're all on the same side, working toward a common goal.

"I lived with hate for a while after this." I gave the scarred stump a light slap with my hand, and our bear buddy kinked his head to the side. I pointed smoothly across to where Braden stood.

"That guy there," I said. "He's the one who pulled me back from the edge."

Bear-boy turned and looked at Braden.

My mate.

My family.

I tensed up, ready to step between them if anything went wrong, but all that happened was the guy seemed to relax.

His fur gradually receded, and he shrank down into human form. When he stood, he was still twitching and scratching. A real loose cannon, but at least he was a more manageable size.

"What is it you need, brother?" I asked him.

"Uh..." He flinched from something only he could see. "Just wanna be... be left alone."

"You know where you are?"

"Of course!"

I tensed, ready to shift in an instant, banking on the chance I could become wolf faster than he could become bear.

"I mean..." the guy continued. "I'm... I think this is..."

I took a long, slow breath as I channeled Braden. I couldn't even tell now if my mate was connecting with me again, or if I'd just absorbed the man's nature enough to mimic him. All I did was think back to that first time we met, when he defused a situation that threatened to explode. And he did it with nothing but well-chosen words.

"This is Gray Vale, brother. Does that help?"

"Gray Vale?"

"And that was a school outing you just scared the hell out of." He looked just as confused then as he had in bear form, so I pushed it a little. "You really worried about what a bunch of little kids can do? They haven't even become, yet."

"Didn't mean... they were on my turf."

There was no point arguing whose turf we were standing on. Instead, I stepped in closer, until I was just about eye to eye with him. "What is it you need, big guy?"

He scratched at his arms, his neck, his face. He flicked his head like he was shooing flies. I was no expert but I figured he was probably a meth head. Why the hell he'd ended up in Burton's Clearing, or in Gray Vale at all, I couldn't even begin to guess.

What mattered most was getting him to stay calm, and taken care of. And it felt as if I'd got that mostly done.

Right up until a half dozen guards came plowing out of the scrub, armed and shouting.

And our big buddy reacted pretty much the same way I always had when confronted by danger, uncertainty or confusion.

He shifted.

CHAPTER FIFTEEN

Braden

IT WASN'T MY place to say it, or my right to feel it, but I was so damn proud of Marius. The way he'd suppressed his natural aggression and looked for a peaceful solution had my heart aching with love for the guy, despite the fact he'd made it clear we couldn't be together.

Not now.

Probably not ever.

The fact he'd also faced down a bear shifter without even looking for vengeance by proxy was even more inspiring. Even when he was still hurting after losing his arm, and by extension the career he'd hoped would last forever. I wouldn't have been surprised if Marius had just said fuck it and gone rogue himself on the massive guy's ass.

Then, when the guards came charging in, and the stranger shifted back into bear form, suddenly it seemed it had all been for nothing. As enormous as Marius was, the immense furry form of the addled shifter dwarfed him.

If my mate had chosen to shift as well, I would have understood it completely. There were six adult wolves here, all males, and together we could at least see this guy off, if not subdue him.

But Marius held out his hand and his damaged arm toward the guards.

"Wait."

"Get out of the way, Ridgie."

Marius shook his head and looked with scorn at Simon, the guard. "Really? You're still holding on to that?"

Simon nodded toward the scarred stump of Marius's left arm. "We can see how well you handle bear shifters, asshole. Let the professionals take over."

A low snarling sound filled the clearing, catching us all by surprise. Most of all me, even though—or really, *because*—I was the one making it.

"Oh, what, Braidy-cat? You're gonna be a fuckin' hero now?"

"You don't know what I'm capable of, Simon, when the people I love are under attack.”

The guardsman just shrugged and turned back to the main event. The bear shifter who was on his hind legs, casting his head side to side. Whether he was looking for escape, looking for drugs, or just seeing pixies, I couldn't tell.

The only two things I was certain of were that he was dangerous... and that my mate was right there in the firing line.

“Hey,” Marius said, waving his hand to get the bear's attention. “Brutus. Down here.”

Somehow, he got through to the guy. Bear-boy glanced down at my man, who still had his hand held up.

“Yeah... remember me? I'm still here. Let's just take a breath, huh?” He nodded toward the two pairs of guards, either side of the clearing. “These guys are ready to fuck you up, man. We can't take any chances with you, y'understand? We all know what a bear can do. *I* sure do, anyway."

The bear snuffled and flinched away from a few more invisible specters. Marius stepped in even closer, making my heart ache and my breath freeze in my throat.

"Can we... can we bring it back down? As badass as you are, man, these guards are armed. They're trained, and they're ready. They're good men. Don't make 'em do bad shit."

The bear opened his mouth wide, and for a moment, I swore he was about to take Marius's head off, even with that scattered assortment of teeth he still had. Instead, he flapped his tongue a moment, and then came down onto all fours.

Marius reached forward, slow as

molasses, and did to the guy exactly what I did that first night to calm my mate. He worked his hand over the bear's big, round head, and scratched him behind the ear.

"It's all cool, Brutus. There's no stranger danger here, buddy. We're all just friends you haven't met."

Christ, I almost burst out in laughter at that. It was absolutely the least *Marius* thing I'd ever heard the man say. Somehow, though, it worked.

Once again, the giant bear's fur receded, his claws and fangs shrank, and he came back down into human form.

He was clearly still scared and confused, but now he could add exhausted to the list. Shifting took a ton of effort every time. To do it so many times in such a short period was bound to have an effect.

The guards came in closer, ready to use their weapons, but the guy gradually came up to his feet. "Don't want trouble."

Marius put his hand around the back of the guy's neck and pulled forward, until their foreheads met with a dull thud. I thought at first he was trying to head butt the guy, until I realized he was connecting with him.

"I've been where you are, buddy. Alone. Scared. Fucking lost."

"Just need a hit."

"I get it." My mate stepped back and Simon and the guardsmen shifted in closer at a cautious pace. "These guys are gonna get you some help. They might need to restrain you. We cool?"

Bear boy nodded and repeated the words that seemed to be his mantra.

"Don't want trouble."

The guardsmen clasped the heavy duty cuffs on him and led him away. Finally, I felt safe to move, and I rushed over to Marius, throwing my arms around him from behind.

Simon paused at the edge of the clearing, barely glancing back over his shoulder before talking.

"Y'did good, Ridgie."

Before either of us could reply, the man simply walked away.

I gripped Marius by the good arm and pulled, trying to turn him to face me. Of course, the big lug resisted like hell, so I moved around in front of him instead.

"What the fuck was that? Do you have a fucking death wish?" I wasn't truly angry, but all the tension inside me had to come out somehow. That was the path it chose.

Marius glared down at me, his eyes bright and intense. I tried to block out the emotion flooding through my mate mark, because it felt too much like fucking stupid fucking *love*. No way I was strong enough to resist that, and absolutely no fucking way I'd survive if he dangled it before me and then pulled it away again.

"Well?" I continued. "Got anything to say, you fucker?" I even slammed the heels of my hands into his bull chest, which pushed me backward, rather than him.

"Not a thing," he murmured. I was just about to swing at the guy when he pulled me in close and slammed his beautiful hard mouth into mine.

My entire body—both parts, the man and the wolf—turned to soft, hot liquid.

All except my cock, which grew so hard, so fast, I thought it might burst.

Marius opened up and danced his tongue past my lips, and let our connection speak for him. My mate mark absorbed every thought, every feeling, every sensation, and pumped it through my body in a heated rush. Apology, loneliness, regret, need.

Destiny.

My mark tingled so hard it burned me, and so help me, it truly was love between the two of us. This big, beautiful bastard had gone and made me fall in love with him, and there wasn't a single damn thing I could do about it.

I pushed myself back out of his embrace, just to catch my breath. To give my soul a chance of surviving if he let fear get the better of him once again, and pulled away from me.

"Braden..."

"Don't start anything you can't—or won't—finish, Marius. So help me, I'll wolf up and I'll bite something else off you. And it won't be your damn hand."

To my surprise, he paused... and then he burst out with laughter. Maybe that was just his tension escaping, but it lit the man up like a firework, and my entire being ached for him.

"Fuck, I've missed you," he said, and it just about cut my legs out from under me.

"I mean it, man. Don't fucking... don't you..." My wolf had too much control to allow me to speak. It prowled and circled inside me, huffing and brushing under my skin, far closer to the surface than I'd have liked. My beast was ready to spring into action at a moment's notice.

"Braden, please. I'm sorry. Shit happened so fucking fast, and... Jesus, I still don't have a handle on simply being a good man, let alone a father. Now suddenly, I'm gay?"

My mark transmitted to him everything I was feeling. Doubt, fear, the beginning of scorn.

"No, no," he said, holding out his hand. "I am. I definitely *am* gay. It's just... it's a lot, y'know?"

It *was* a lot. Even when the two clans were separated, and Gray Vale was the more open and understanding place, it was hard at first to be open. I couldn't imagine how it must be for Marius, with all his background and baggage, to have his sexuality basically body slam him from out of the shadows.

"Yeah," I said. "I know. But our secret ain't all that secret, anymore. It's kinda well and truly out there now. So the question is more about how you deal with that."

He pulled me right in against his thick chest and kissed the top of my head. "Come home with me. Let me show you how I plan to deal with it."

CHAPTER SIXTEEN

Marius

I THOUGHT ALL the children and teachers would've gone back to the school, but they were waiting in the clearing between the forest and the town. The moment we stepped out of the tree cover, Noah broke away from his class and ran over to us.

And to my surprise and delight, he

came straight to me. If I was honest, I'd expected him to run to Braden, instead. And it wouldn't have bothered me, since the man is my mate. Still, my heart swelled, and it was like a bear shifter in my chest. I swore it was too big, about to explode.

As I picked my beautiful son up and hugged him to me, and Braden put his arms around me from behind, I finally understood what it meant to be home.

To be loved.

Others tried to talk to me as we walked through town but I couldn't focus on them. Couldn't even hear them. I was too busy with my son and my mate.

My family.

The walk home passed in a blur as Noah snuggled against me and Braden used our connection to send me all kinds of warm and loving vibes. I managed to hold my son in my damaged arm, which meant I could put my other arm around my mate, and caress the mark I'd given him.

As we walked into my shitty little apartment, I realized it had never looked more like a home to me. And it was because of who was there with me, and nothing else.

Exhaustion overtook Noah in a rush, so we made a quick and simple dinner, and then together, my mate and I tucked the kid into bed.

After Braden kissed my son's forehead and left, I stroked my fingers back through the Noah's hair. Something I didn't remember ever doing before. The kind of casual affection that had been missing from my life, and as a consequence, from my kid's.

My boy went out like a light, and that bear shifter in my chest made it damn hard to breathe. Fuck... apparently unconditional love is both a killer, and also everything I'd ever wanted to live for.

I quietly closed Noah's bedroom door as I left the room. Something I usually didn't do, out of fear. So he could get to me, or I could get to him, with as little trouble as possible. In case he had nightmares, or called out for his mom. Or in case I needed to look in on him to reassure myself he was still actually there. That he wasn't some little angel who only existed in my dreams.

But this time, I knew I needed it closed. The things I was about to do to Braden... those needed to be done without interruption.

HIS WOUNDED WARRIOR

***

He was waiting for me in my bedroom. We'd been naked from when we shifted until we got back into the apartment, where we'd just put robes on. Somehow, his nakedness in that moment on my bed was different. Before, it was just the absence of clothing.

Now, it was a promise.

I strode over to him and shoved him straight down onto my bed, diving on over the top of him. He came up to meet me, plowing his mouth into mine and hauling on my tongue as he made hard fists in my hair.

Braden snapped his legs around my back and pulled down on my hips, driving us together, grinding his hard, swollen cock against mine. His rich scent poured into my entire being, filling me—mind, heart and soul—like nothing ever had.

I slid my mouth down to that mark I had given him. It had healed up into a scar, but it glowed red and burned as I traced it with my tongue. Braden kinked his head away to bare himself fully to me, and it took all my strength to stop myself from reopening that beautiful wound.

Still, Braden squeezed me in the sizzling embrace of his legs. My cock wrestled with his, driving lightning bolts of bliss racing through my body. His mate mark crackled as the sensations passed between us, until I couldn't tell what was his pleasure and what was mine.

My hunger for every part him, body and soul, had my wolf bristling, prowling, demanding succor. Braden's essence called to me, through my nose and through my mouth.

I slid lower, lapping at this beautiful man's chest, swamping his nipple with the wet heat of my tongue. His moans became growls as I bit down on his tight bud, and his whole body jerked when I curled my hand around his cock.

My ravenous need for him overtook me for a moment. It felt for all the world like I imagine madness would.

Wolf and man trying to coexist in a single space and time.

My skin prickled as if readying for a shift. Preparing me for thick fur to come bursting out.

I slid lower and drove my mouth down the length of Braden's thick, engorged cock, growling with sweet contentment as his essence burst across my tongue and I finally tasted my mate again.

He tightened his grip on my hair and arched his back, pumping his hips at me as I swallowed every long, spicy inch of him.

Harder, faster, I stroked up and down his length, gripping his balls and squeezing lightly, wishing more than ever that I had my other hand so I could grind at his ass.

"Fuck... Marius..."

Jesus, the yearning in his voice nearly made me come. I needed to be inside him, as soon as fucking possible.

I released his balls and slid my hand up to his mouth. He sucked on my thumb for a moment, understanding exactly what I needed without me even asking.

With my thumb all slicked up, I brought it back down and pressed it to Braden's tight ass. He hauled his legs higher and wider, and I made hard circles around his rippled ring, then punched the tip of my digit inside him.

My mate hissed with sheer desire, and his cock pulsed hard in my mouth. I drank down his salty precum and worked more and more of my thumb inside his tight hole.

"Uhhh..." Braden was so close to coming, and though a part of me wanted to edge him, most of me—the wolf side of me—had no fucking patience. Both sides of me needed to finish him right now. Out of desire, out of apology... more than anything, out of love.

Braden hissed and slammed his hands down on my shoulders, hard enough to sting. He dug his lengthening nails into my flesh, and roared with his release as he arched his back and filled my mouth with his musky fluid. As tempting as it was to swallow, to take him into me like that, instead, I held his essence inside me for a moment.

God, it was fucking perfect.

He was still pulsing when I dragged my thumb out and sat up, letting my mate's cum drizzle out into my palm. I coated his ass and my cock with his slick juice, and notched myself in place.

There was no waiting. Nothing subtle. This was fucking beastly. As close as I'd ever been to my animal form without actually shifting.

Mentally, I was more wolf than man. Physically, I was teetering.

A different kind of edge play.

It would take so little for me to relax into a shift, and it was taking so fucking much willpower to stay human.

When I drove my hips forward, Braden cried out with the sweet stinging agony of my thick cock filling him. He whipped his hands up around the back of my head and hauled me down.

I slammed my mouth into his, tasting the fresh salty wonder of blood as I punched my cock in and out of him. My mate squeezed me deep inside his body, as if holding me tight, as if crying out for me to stay there, to never leave.

The heat in my mind cascaded down through my body, as the fire deep in my cock rose. They met in the middle and formed a solid force that punched against the inside of my chest, in the form of my wild fucking heart. Reaching out for Braden.

As I glided in and out of him, I snaked my one good hand down beneath his gorgeous body and held him close. Mouth to mouth, chest to chest, soul to soul. His heart knocked against the wall of his ribs, like Morse code, and mine answered. It was a language neither of us had ever heard, but which both of us understood completely.

I slid my mouth down to Braden's neck, and clamped tight over his mark. An instant later, my mate completed the bond, embedding his partially-shifted fangs into my shoulder, sinking them so deep it was as if he was part of me physically. Like he already was, emotionally.

His sweet, spicy blood flooded my mouth, and mine his. A cycle of giving and receiving, of exchanging souls, pumped fiercely through both of us. I'd heard about those sensations and always thought they were fairytales. Only in the moment did I understand the stories didn't even come close to the truth.

With one long, ferocious pump of my hips, I reached a cyclonic climax, made stronger, hotter, wetter by the sharing of blood and souls as much as from the physical sensation of being so deeply embedded in, and connected with, my lover's body.

Braden snarled, his voice grinding against the skin of my neck, as he reached another climax, bursting between our bodies. The sweet heat of his release coated my belly and his, as my own juice erupted within him.

I gradually slowed to a halt, still inside him, still hard as fuck. Seated within his body as he was seated within my heart. I didn't want to pull out.

Not fucking ever.

"I don't want that, either," Braden murmured, his lips still pressed to my skin as our shared marks confessed all my thoughts to him, and his to me.

I had the feeling this would be one long, strenuous night. The first night of forever with this beautiful man.

EPILOGUE

One Year Later...
Braden

I HELD MARIUS close, emotional tears stinging the backs of my eyes as we both waved to Noah, heading in for his first day in first grade. As great as things had been in the last school year, I just knew it was going to get even better from that point on.

After that first night, way back, when Marius took my mark and reconnected us, life had bloomed into pure happiness.

We'd finally fallen asleep in the early morning, after hours of blissful fucking, only to be awoken by Noah at sunrise. And as I'd hoped and believed, the boy had absolutely no trouble dealing with the whole thing. His father and his schoolteacher were sharing a bed. So what. It was time for breakfast. That was all that mattered to him at that point.

Turned out, Noah's wolf senses were a little precocious. He'd already scented me on his dad, and vice versa, long before he found us together.

Thankfully, they both agreed to move in with me, since my place was bigger and... well, frankly, Marius wouldn't know decor if it bit his other hand off.

HIS WOUNDED WARRIOR

Having two parents had suited Noah so well. Yeah, so, it was two dads where all his friends had moms. I'd always radiated a bit of mom-energy, anyway, despite being a dude.

The fact that nobody in all of Gray Vale blinked an eye at it was a bonus, but I knew Noah well enough now to realize he wouldn't have been bothered either way.

It had been almost impossible to separate my role as the school's kindergarten teacher from my role as a step dad to Noah. Days like this one were the hardest, since I had to leave him and go teach my own group of kids.

Even so, my heart swelled with pride, and reached out to Marius, who kissed the top of my head, the way he always did when I got all soppy.

"You're such a pussy, Bray."

"And you're just a big, horrible, smelly, ugly oaf," I said, digging my elbow into his ribs.

"Hey," he replied, tightening his arm around my neck. "I'm not ugly."

I turned in his embrace, and framed his face with my hands. "Hell no, you're not. But the rest is still true."

He smiled for a moment, before coming forward to kiss me, gliding his tongue into my mouth before I could even prepare.

Sparks ignited over every inch of my skin, like a shift beginning, and I almost lost myself in this huge, gorgeous man. Yet again.

"Dammit, man," I said, and shoved him in his chest. Of course, as always, the sheer size of the man meant all I managed was to push myself back from him. "Don't you fucking dare. I have a class to teach.”

“Well, fine,” he murmured. “I'll hold the rest of it for when you get home, handsome.”

“I'll hold you to that,” I said, flashing him a sultry grin as I smacked his ass cheek.

***

Thank you for reading His Wounded Warrior. If you enjoyed this book, please do me a favor and leave me a review. I do read them, and even a few positive words will help me in crafting more of the books my readers love.

Thank you!

~Evie Riley

Turn the page to read a preview of Mason, Book 1 in the Federal Protection Agency series.

PREVIEW

Mason

POSTTRAUMATIC STRESS DISORDER is a psychiatric disorder that may occur in people who have experienced or witnessed a traumatic event such as a natural disaster, a serious accident, a terrorist act, war/combat, or rape, or who have been threatened with death, sexual violence, or serious injury. Symptoms include: intrusive thoughts, nightmares, avoiding reminders of the event, memory loss, negative thoughts about self and the world, self-isolation, feeling distant, anger and irritability, reduced interest in favorite activities, hyper vigilance, difficulty concentrating, insomnia, vivid flashbacks, avoiding people, places and things related to the event, casting blame, difficulty feeling positive emotions, exaggerated startle response, and risky behaviors.

"What a bunch of bullshit," I said, and tossed my phone onto the dash of my rental truck.

The shrink I had hired to help me with my insomnia had just diagnosed me with PTSD and it was a load of shit. Just because I had some of the symptoms, didn't mean that was what was wrong with me.

I was able to function.

I was doing my job.

I just had some problems outside of it.

I was having a hard time sleeping, and when I did, I usually had nightmares. I was a bit on edge, but never in the field. I wasn't angry or lashing out at people. I wasn't having flashbacks or panic attacks. Sure, at times, I had a hard time sitting still. I got anxious sometimes at night but I would just go for a run with Koda and I was fine.

I didn't have PTSD.

Besides, I didn't even know where it would have come from. I was a federal agent with Homeland security. I specialized in crimes against children and, yes, I saw some horrific things, but nothing that the other Agents hadn't already seen.

Agents that had been on the job for twenty years were fine with the things we see, so how could that give me PTSD when it didn't with others?

The shrink was wrong. It was just that simple. Everyone struggled with sleeping from time to time.

And if I had to have a few drinks in the day to get through the night, then so what?

I never drank while on duty. It was always after work. I wasn't drinking an excessive amount, just enough to help me fall asleep when it had been a few days. I was coping and there was nothing wrong with it.

Koda whined beside me and I glanced over at him. Koda was my K9 partner, a beautiful German shepherd.

I loved this dog.

I didn't know what I would do without him.

I've always loved dogs and when the opportunity presented itself for me to be a K9 handler five years ago, I jumped at the chance. I've had Koda ever since he was an eight week old puppy, and I couldn't imagine not having him in my life.

My greatest fear is for Koda to be hurt in the field.

"You want to go and see Uncle Ro?" I asked the dog as I started to pet him. I was currently sitting in my rental truck out front of my older brother's house.

Roland, or Ro as I always called him, was a local cop. He was also ex-military and had been a cop in New York City before he moved out here. I was surprised when he decided to move to a smaller town like Gaithersburg, but it was his life and he was free to do with it as he wished.

He knew I was coming by, that I had taken some vacation days. He didn't know about the real troubles I'd been having with my sleep. I wasn't about to tell him and add to his own worries and stress.

Letting out yet another sigh, I removed my seatbelt and got out. I might as well get this over and done with. The second we opened the door and strolled inside, Koda ran right toward the kitchen where I knew Roland would be.

"Hello, my sweet boy," Roland said as he started to pet Koda. "You know he loves me better, right?" he teased as he looked right at me.

I couldn't help but roll my eyes.

"He only likes you because you slip him food from the table when you think

I'm not looking."

Roland was terrible at keeping Koda on his proper diet and schedule. He was always slipping him people food, even when he knew he wasn't supposed to be. It wasn't that Koda couldn't have a treat, but he had to earn it. He needed to work for it. That wasn't my rule, it was the rule for all of the working dogs.

"How was the trip?" Roland asked as he reluctantly moved away from Koda and opened his arms to give me a hug.

Roland was massive. It never failed to gain attention. He was twice my size and I wasn't a small guy. I had muscles and was more than capable of holding my own in a fight.

Roland had taught me how to fight. When I decided I wanted to be a federal agent, Roland had made sure I would be able to handle anything that came my way. He trained me in multiple fighting styles and shooting. He made sure I was ready for any fight.

We had a similar look, though, in terms of hair, eye color, and the shape of our face. You could tell by looking at us that we were brothers. We were both good looking and both gay. Though, unlike me, Roland took a long time to come out.

"Not bad. Airplanes are nothing for me. So what's been going on since we last spoke? You seem to be in a better mood than you were a few days ago. I expected to find you on the couch in sweatpants with empty pizza boxes and beer cans all around you."

When we had last talked, Roland was in a dark place. The guy that he liked, Tyler, hadn't spoken to him in a couple of weeks. He had also taken a week off of work.

It was the first time he had truly liked another guy since he had lost Shane. Shane was the man that he was madly in love with when he was younger and still in the Army.

Shane was out and proud, but Roland had been afraid to come out. Don't Ask, Don't Tell, was no longer in effect, but that didn't mean an organization flooded with alpha males would be open-minded about serving next to a gay man.

Roland had stayed in the closet and there was only so long Shane could handle it. One night, after an epic fight, Shane stormed off in the car, only to be hit by a drunk driver. Shane died on impact and the drunk driver got away. Roland then quit the Army and joined the

NYPD. He was the one that caught his lover's killer a few years later. Roland hadn't been in a relationship with anyone since.

"Tyler came over last night. We had a great conversation," he said, and flashed a warm smile.

"Oh, just a conversation?" I teased as I grabbed some coffee and headed for the table.

"A bit more than that. It started off with a conversation. He told me that he needed time to get his feelings in order and to process everything that had just happened."

"Makes sense, he thought he was straight his whole life. Having a guy kiss you out of nowhere can be shocking," I said with complete understanding to my voice.

"And that was my fault for doing it that way. It came out of nowhere. Thankfully, though, I didn't scare him off for very long. He told me he had feelings for me, too. That he didn't even sleep with the two women he had been dating in the past two months. He's actually never slept with a woman before, or anyone."

"Damn, you bagged yourself a twenty-two year old virgin. Now I'm jealous."

I was a sucker for a virgin or a spinner. I liked the smaller guys, the ones that you could toss around and overpower. I wasn't a fan of vanilla sex. I liked to have power over my lover. I liked to use toys and restraints. Sex was supposed to be fun and I believed in trying many different flavors of it. I tended to go for smaller guys, because they loved to bottom and I was only a top.

"The point is, we are taking things slow. We watched a movie and made out a bit last night before we went to sleep, in separate rooms. I'm trying to make him feel comfortable and allow him to stay in control of the sexual progress."

"I am happy for you. It's been a very long time since you've allowed yourself to be with another man. I know what happened with Shane was devastating, but you've kinda been putting your whole life on pause, Ro. I don't know what it's like to lose the man you love, and I didn't know him as well as I should have, but he wouldn't want this for you. He wouldn't want you to be alone and heartbroken for the rest of your life."

"I'm trying. What about you? Any new guy in your life?"

"Not right now, no. I've been too busy

with work. I'm not really the dating type, anyway. It's easier to keep things to friends with benefits or one-night stands."

I held zero interest in dating someone. With my job, it really wasn't even possible. I worked too many hours and I traveled all over the country at a moment's notice. It wasn't conducive to a healthy relationship.

"Always such a romantic," Roland teased, and once again I rolled my eyes.

Before I could comment, Koda's head snapped up and he looked right at the door. Instantly, I was on edge and ready for an attack. I knew it wasn't a normal reaction, but it was what always happened, now, when there was a knock at the door or the phone rang. I was always ready for an ambush and there was nothing I could do about it.

"You expecting someone?" I asked, doing my best to keep my voice calm and casual. I wasn't sure if I was able to pull it off.

"It's Isaiah, my friend with Social Services. He's coming by so we can talk about the foster home situation," Roland answered as he got up to let him in.

Roland had told me about Tyler, his current love interest, and his old partner, Jasper Monroe's reaction to each other. When he told me that Tyler seemed scared of his old foster father, I could tell it was bothering him.

Tyler had grown up in the foster care system and, for a couple of years, he'd had Monroe as his foster father. Monroe had never told Roland about it, not even after him and Tyler started to hang out. We both found their reactions to each other suspicious and decided that it should be looked into.

It wasn't common for a former foster child to have that much fear toward a foster father. Something had to have happened and I was worried what it was. I didn't want my brother to be caught in a deadly situation if it came back that Monroe was a dirty cop.

"Hey man, come on in," Roland said warmly as he opened the door.

I peaked around the corner so I could see what Isaiah looked like. I don't know what I was expecting for Isaiah, but I wasn't expecting what stood on the other side of the door. The man was a bit chubby and average looking, probably a teddy bear, but he looked like a wreck. Like he hadn't slept in days. I wasn't sure, but something was going on with him.

"Is your brother here?" he asked as he walked in.

"Yeah, in the kitchen. Come on back and grab a coffee. You look like you could use it."

"You wouldn't believe what I found, Roland," he said as they ambled toward the kitchen.

I had no idea what he had found, but by how he was behaving, he found something huge.

My gut said it was something I wasn't going to like.

"Mason, this is Isaiah. He works with Social Services and is who I reached out to about intel on Tyler," Roland said to me.

"It's nice to meet you," I said as I held my hand out for Isaiah to take.

He easily clasped my hand in his

before he spoke.

"Nice to meet you. I have a feeling we're going to need your help on this one."

I didn't like the sound of that. It was one thing to need a cop, but to need a federal agent, that meant something huge had happened.

"What did you find?" Roland asked, getting things started.

"I started by looking through Tyler's time with Jasper. As you know, he was there between the ages of twelve and fourteen. He was one of eight foster kids, sometimes a little less over the two years. On the surface, it all seems perfectly normal and there weren't any red flags in Tyler's file for Jasper. Before that, he had been through a lot of rough homes and had been abused. It all stopped for two years before he was sent to another foster home, and then it picked up all over again."

"Okay, but I'm not hearing anything to imply that something is wrong with Jasper. Sounds like you need to review all of the foster homes in the system, though," I said.

It wasn't uncommon for there to be a few bad apples within the foster home system. However, it sounded like they had more than a couple in this town.

"Tyler was diagnosed with a protein deficiency when he was eight. It makes it hard for him to gain weight. Aside from that, and the asthma, he was perfectly healthy. Broken bones and bruising, but no illnesses. For the two years he was with Jasper, everything was perfect. Too perfect. Bruises were gone, he went to school, everything was normal and without complaint. Then, all of a sudden, he is being transferred, by Jasper's request to another home and the hell started all over again. Only, he was there for two days when he started to get very sick. His social worker saw how sick he was and took him to the hospital. They ran his bloodwork and discovered he was going through cocaine withdrawal."

"Whoa, what?" Roland asked, shocked and outraged.

That wasn't good.

That confirmed that something more was going on within that foster home and it wasn't going to end well.

"There was no way of telling how it got into his system, just that it was there. His social worker asked where he got the drugs, but he clammed up. Jasper was brought in to be questioned, but he was a Detective, even back then, so the worker believed everything he said. He said Tyler must have gotten it from school, that he had no idea. They went with Jasper's story and never looked into his home or any of the other children."

"It's not uncommon for children in their young teenage years to get their hands on cocaine. I find it hard to believe that no one would have noticed. If he was going through physical withdrawals, he had to have been doing it for months and in large doses. Were any of the other children checked out?" I asked.

"That's the thing, the social worker never spoke to any of the current children or looked through his home. So, I did." He placed a rather large brown file on the table as he continued. "That is Jasper's and his wife, Dana's, fostering file. It includes every child they have ever taken in, including the current ones. Currently, he has nine kids all between the ages of nine and fourteen. I've started to go through the process of pulling the previous foster children's files, but there are over a hundred and fifty of them."

"Shit," Roland said, obviously shocked that it was that many.

That *was* a fast turnaround.

I knew that some homes kids came and went at one hell of a pace, however, that was usually in larger cities. The smaller cities, the kids tended to stay with their one foster parent unless something was wrong with them. Kids didn't tend to get passed around like Christmas candy in towns this size, as a general rule. There was no reason for Monroe to have that many previous children.

I was getting a bad feeling about this and it wasn't going to end well. Monroe was Roland's past partner. They were still partners when they needed backup on a case. This wasn't going to go well if Monroe was dirty, and it was starting to look like he was.

"It's going to take some time to pull all of their files and go through them to see if any doctor reports were made after their time with Jasper. Some were also moved to another city and I don't have access to their files," Isaiah continued.

"I can get 'em. I just need their names and I can pull the file, no matter where they were placed in the country. We need to do a sneak and peek at Monroe's house and see what is going on. I'm assuming you are operating under the impression that Monroe is cooking drugs in the house," I stated.

I had come here for a vacation, but I also knew that Roland was worried about Tyler. It was the least I could do after everything my brother had done for me.

"Last night, I looked through twenty files. Twelve of the kids were admitted to the hospital with withdrawal-like symptoms. Not all of them were given blood work. Most were told it was the flu and they would feel better in a few days. It's enough for me to make the hypothesis that cocaine is being either cooked at the house around the children, or the children were weighing and packaging the cocaine."

"That sounds like a reasonable hypothesis. I've never noticed any problems with Jasper being sick, though, in three years," Roland stated.

"Depends. I've gone into a lot of homes where the drugs were made in the basement and the kids were sick but the foster parents weren't. The kids were the ones touching the drugs and breathing it in as they were either cooking or packaging it. The parents were fine, because the ventilation system in the upstairs of the house was solid. It kept the fumes down in the basement and when they needed to go down there, they wore the proper protection. It's completely logical that Monroe isn't breathing it in. Just like it's logical that he is breathing it in, but he's never not been around it. His body could be addicted to it and he gets his fix by being in the house," I pointed out.

"Let's get the files and go through

them. See which kids were hospitalized after leaving Jasper's. I'll loop in Captain Perry so he's aware of the situation. Yes, we'll need to do a sneak and peek at his house. Mase, can you get a warrant from a judge? We gotta keep that out of town."

"I'll get it. With those files, we should have enough for a warrant," I said confidently. That was easy enough to do and I agreed that it needed to be out of town. A town this size, everyone knew everyone and no judge was going to give us a sneak and peek warrant with what we had.

"Okay, I have to go to the office and start pulling them. Do you want to join me there, or do you want me to bring them back here?" Isaiah asked.

"It would be better to do it here. We don't know who will talk to who. I want to try and keep this as quiet as possible," Roland answered.

"I'll be back in about an hour or so, then," Isaiah said, before he finished his coffee and headed out.

"I'll grab my bag and get my laptop out of it. I'll get A.S.A Crawford up to speed and he'll grab us a warrant," I said as I stood.

"Not exactly the vacation you were looking for. I'm sorry."

"It's okay. The drug cases are the easiest. Have you thought about just asking Tyler again? Tell him you know that Jasper could be mixed up with drugs."

It would make things easier if he talked to Tyler about it. It was most likely the reason why Tyler didn't want to talk about Monroe. That old fear was still inside of him, but if Roland could get him to open up, it would help a lot.

I might not be able to get a sneak and peek warrant with what we had. We might need Tyler to go on the record about what happened in that house to do something about it.

"No, I want to keep him out of this. I don't know what is going on, but I know that when drug dealers feel threatened, they'll attack the one they feel is responsible. I don't want Tyler getting hurt. It's better to leave him in the dark."

"It's your call. I'll support you in whatever you decide, Ro. I'll go grab my gear," I said with complete understanding to my voice.

I knew how dangerous drug dealers could be, especially with children. If he didn't want to bring Tyler into this just yet, that was his call and I would respect it.

Hopefully, we wouldn't need Tyler and I could secure us a warrant without anyone on record.

One thing was for certain, this wasn't the type of vacation I had been planning.

For more of Mason and the FPA, please visit your favorite online retailer and grab your copy!

OTHER BOOKS BY EVIE

Federal Protection Agency
Mason
Rafe
Ryzen
Cooper
Noah
Damien
Sebastian
Gabe
Logan

Ruthless Empire
Courting Danger
Chasing Danger
Kissing Danger

Smokejumpers
Hawke
Cyrus
Jase
Gage
Jackson
Xavier

Jasper Springs
Cade
Dawson
Drew
Grayson
Riley
Mitch

From The Edge
Shattered
Runaway
Jaded
Rescue
Hidden
Tormented

Gray Vale Pack
His Fated Mate
His Wounded Warrior
His Healing Heart

ABOUT THE AUTHOR

Evie Riley is a prolific, neurodivergent author known for her captivating MM romance novels. She has gained a significant following and topped the LGBT+ action and adventure bestseller charts with her series.

Evie's writing style often explores dark and gritty themes where her men must overcome difficult obstacles in their search for love, but she has also ventured into sweeter small-town romances, incorporating tropes like enemies-to-lovers, friends-to-lovers, age-gap, and forced proximity. She is known for crafting engaging romantic suspense novels and has a knack for creating interconnected series worlds that keep readers invested.

Interestingly, Ms. Riley has hinted at exploring new genres, such as Alien Omegaverse Romance, in the future.

Outside of writing, she enjoys spending time at the beach and has a quirky personality, described by her partner as ranging from cute to deadly, depending on her blood-chocolate levels.

Evie spends her nights writing bad boys in love, and her days wrangling the sweet boys she loves.